By Ira Levin

PLAYS

Deathtrap
Veronica's Room
Break a Leg
Dr. Cook's Garden
Drat! The Cat!
Critic's Choice
General Seeger
Interlock
No Time for Sergeants
(from the novel by Mac Hyman)

NOVELS

The Boys from Brazil
The Stepford Wives
This Perfect Day
Rosemary's Baby
A Kiss Before Dying

DEATHTRAP

DEATHTRAP

A THRILLER IN TWO ACTS

IRA LEVIN

RANDOM HOUSE   NEW YORK

Library of Congress Cataloging in Publication Data
Levin, Ira.
    Deathtrap : a thriller in two acts.

    I. Title.
PS3523.E7993D4   812'.5'4   78–57128
ISBN 0–394–50727–4

Manufactured in the United States of America
9 8 7 6 5 4 3 2
First Edition

To Phyllis

DEATHTRAP *was first presented on February 26, 1978, by Alfred de Liagre, Jr., and Roger L. Stevens at The Music Box Theater in New York City with the following cast:*

(In order of appearance)

SIDNEY BRUHL	John Wood
MYRA BRUHL	Marian Seldes
CLIFFORD ANDERSON	Victor Garber
HELGA TEN DORP	Marian Winters
PORTER MILGRIM	Richard Woods

Directed by Robert Moore
Scenery by William Ritman
Costumes by Ruth Morley
Lighting by Marc B. Weiss

THE SCENE

The action takes place in Sidney Bruhl's study, in the Bruhl home in Westport, Connecticut.

ACT ONE
SCENE ONE: An afternoon in October.
SCENE TWO: That evening.
SCENE THREE: Two hours later.

ACT TWO
SCENE ONE: Two weeks later, morning.
SCENE TWO: A week later, night.
SCENE THREE: A week later, afternoon.

ACT
ONE

SIDNEY BRUHL'*s study is a handsomely converted stable grafted onto an authentically Colonial house. Sliding doors upstage center open on a foyer in which are the house's front door, entrances to the living room and kitchen, and the stairway to the second floor. French doors upstage right open out to a shrubbery-flanked patio. Downstage left is a fieldstone fireplace, practical to the extent that paper can be burned in it.*

*Except for the bookshelves and some inconspicuous two-drawer file cabinets, the room's furnishings are tastefully chosen antiques: a few chairs and occasional pieces, a buffet downstage right with liquor decanters, and—the focus of the room—*SIDNEY'S *desk, which is moderately cluttered with papers, reference books, an electric typewriter, a phone. Patterned draperies hang at the French doors. The room is decorated with framed theatrical window cards and a collection of guns, handcuffs, maces, broadswords, and battle-axes.*

When the curtain rises, SIDNEY BRUHL *is seated thoughtfully at his desk. He's about fifty, an impressive and well-tended man, wearing a cardigan sweater over a turtleneck shirt. The typewriter is covered. The draperies are open at the French doors; it's late afternoon of a sunny day in October. The door to the foyer opens partway and* MYRA BRUHL *looks in. She's in her forties, slim and self-effacing, in a sweater and skirt. She enters quietly with an ice bucket, which she places on the buffet.* SIDNEY *notices her.*

3

SIDNEY *Deathtrap.* (MYRA *turns*) A thriller in two acts. One set, five characters. *(Lifts a manuscript in a paperboard binder)* A juicy murder in Act One, unexpected developments in Act Two. Sound construction, good dialogue, laughs in the right places. Highly commercial.

    (He tosses the manuscript on the desk)

MYRA Why, that's *wonderful,* darling! I'm so happy for you! For both of us!

SIDNEY Happy? Why on earth happy?

MYRA But—it's yours, isn't it? The idea you had in August?

SIDNEY The idea I had in August has gone the way of the idea I had in June, and the idea I had in whenever it was before then: in the fireplace, up the chimney, and out over Fairfield County—pollution in its most grisly form. This arrived in the mail this morning. It's the property of one . . . *(Finds the covering letter)* . . . Clifford Anderson. He was one of the twerps at the seminar. *(Reads the letter, twerpishly)* "Dear Mr. Bruhl: I hope you don't mind my sending you my play *Deathtrap,* which I finished retyping at two o'clock this morning. Since I couldn't have written it without the inspiration of your own work and the guidance and encouragement you gave me last summer, I thought it only fitting that you should be the first person to read it. If you find it one tenth as good as any of your own thrillers, I'll consider my time well spent and the fee for the seminar more than adequately recompensed."

MYRA *(Sitting)* *That's* nice.

SIDNEY No it isn't, it's fulsome. "Please excuse the carbon copy; the local Xerox machine is on the fritz, and I couldn't stand the thought of waiting a few days to send my *first-born child* off to its *spiritual father.*" My italics, his emetics. "I hope you'll call or write as soon as you've read it and let me know whether you think it's worthy of submitting to . . ." et cetera, et cetera. Son of a bitch even *types* well. *(Tosses the letter on the desk)* I think I remember him. Enormously obese. A glandular condition. Four hundred pounds . . . I wonder where he got my address.

MYRA From the university?

SIDNEY Probably.
(He rises and heads for the buffet)

MYRA Is it really that good? His first play?

SIDNEY It can't miss. A gifted director couldn't even hurt it. *(Fixing something on the rocks)* It'll run for years. The stock and amateur rights will feed and clothe generations of Andersons. It can *easily* be opened up for a movie. George C. Scott—and Liv Ullmann.

MYRA *(Rising)* And Trish Van Devere.

SIDNEY There's a part in it for her too. The damn thing is perfect.

MYRA I should think you'd be proud that one of your students has written a salable play.

SIDNEY *(Considers her)* For the first time in eleven years of marriage, darling: Drop dead.

MYRA My goodness . . .
(She puts things right at the buffet as SIDNEY *moves away with his drink)*

SIDNEY I'm green with envy. I'd like to beat the wretch over the head with the mace there, bury him in a four-hundred-pound hole somewhere, and send the thing off under my own name. To . . . David Merrick . . . or Hal Prince. *(Thinks a bit, looks at* MYRA*)* Now, *there's* the best idea I've had in ages.

MYRA *(Going to him)* Ah, my poor Sidney . . .
(She hugs him, kisses his cheek)

SIDNEY I mean, what's the point in owning a mace if you don't *use* it once in a while?

MYRA Ah . . . You'll get an idea of your own, any day now, and it'll turn into a better play than that one.

SIDNEY Don't bet on it. Not that you have any money to bet with.

MYRA We're doing very nicely in that department: not one creditor beating at the door.

SIDNEY But for how long? I've just about cleaned you out now, haven't I?

MYRA *We've* cleaned me out, and it's been joy and delight every bit of the way. *(Kisses him)* Your next play will simply have to be a terrific smash.

SIDNEY *(Moving away)* Thanks. That's what I need, an easing of the pressure.
(He moves to the desk, toys with the manuscript)

MYRA Why don't you call it to Merrick's attention? Maybe you could get . . . a commission of some kind.

SIDNEY A finder's fee, you mean?

MYRA If that's what it's called.

SIDNEY A great and glorious one percent. Maybe one and a half.

MYRA Or better yet, why don't you produce it yourself? You've been involved in enough productions to know how to do it. And it might be a beneficial change of pace.

SIDNEY Darling, I may be devious and underhanded enough to be a successful murderer, but not, I think, a Broadway producer. One mustn't overestimate one's talents.

MYRA Collaborate with him. Isn't there room for improvement in the play, good as it is? The professional touch, a little reshaping and sharpening?

SIDNEY *That's* a possibility . . .

MYRA I'm sure he'd be thrilled at the chance to work with you.

SIDNEY   We'd split fifty–fifty . . .

MYRA   And you'd get top billing.

SIDNEY   Naturally. "Reverse alphabetical order, dear boy; it's done all the time."

MYRA   On the basis of *who you are*.

SIDNEY   Sidney Four-Flops Bruhl.

MYRA   Sidney Author-of–*The Murder Game* Bruhl.

SIDNEY   *(A doddering ancient)* "Oh yes, *The Murder Game!* I remember that one. Back in the time of King Arthur, wasn't it?"

MYRA   Not quite that long ago.

SIDNEY   Eighteen years, love. Eighteen years, each one flying faster than the one before. Nothing recedes like success. Mmm, that *is* a good one, isn't it? *(Taking up a memo pad and pen)* Maybe I can work it in someplace. There's a has-been actor who could say it. "Recedes" is e-d-e, right?

MYRA   Yes. You see, you *would* improve it.

SIDNEY   Give it the inimitable Sidney Bruhl flavor. Close in Boston.
    (He puts the pad and pen down, picks up the letter)

MYRA   Call him now. Where does he live?

SIDNEY   Up in Milford. *(Moves around nearer the phone. Studies the letter awhile, looks at MYRA)* You don't like the mace . . .

MYRA   No, definitely not. Blood on the carpet. And the next day Helga ten Dorp would be picking up the psychic vibrations.

SIDNEY   In Holland? I doubt it very much.

MYRA   Sidney, what were you smoking Friday night when the rest of us were smoking grass? She's taken the McBain cottage for six months. Paul Wyman is doing a book with her. He was impersonating her for fifteen minutes.

SIDNEY   Oh. I thought he was finally coming out of the closet.

MYRA   You see what a fine murderer you'd be? Helga ten Dorp moves in practically on your doorstep, and you manage not to hear about it.

SIDNEY   That *does* give one pause.

MYRA   It certainly should. Nan and Tom Wesson had her to dinner last week and she told Tom about his backaches, and the money he put into silver, and his father's thing for tall women. She warned Nan that their *au pair* girl was going to leave, which she did two days later, and she found a set of keys Nan lost in 1969; they were under the clothes dryer.

SIDNEY   Hmm. She's in the McBain cottage?

MYRA   *(Pointing through the French doors)*   Right over yonder. Picking up our blips on her radar this minute, most likely.

SIDNEY Well! It seems that Mr. Anderson has himself a collaborator. Not that I really believe in ESP . . .

MYRA The police in Europe seem to. That's half of why she's here; she's supposed to be resting. From pointing at murderers.

SIDNEY Wait a minute now, the fat one didn't stay the full week, and his name was . . . Quinn or Quincy. Anderson, Anderson. I wonder if he's the one with the awful stammer.

MYRA *(Indicating the phone)* Easy way to find out.

SIDNEY Yes. Hmm. *(Studies the letter for another moment, then puts it down, and referring to it, dials the phone)* This *may* be a three-hour conversation. *(Listens awhile, hangs up)* Busy. Probably talking to Merrick. *(He frowns, waiting with his hand on the phone; sees* MYRA *watching him with concern)* What's for dinner?

MYRA Salmon.

SIDNEY Again?

MYRA Yes . . . Sidney? Would you—actually *kill someone* to have another successful play?

SIDNEY *(Thinks about it)* Don't be foolish, darling. Of course I would. *(Toward the French doors)* Spoken in jest, Miss ten Dorp!

MYRA It's Mrs.; she's divorced.

SIDNEY No wonder. Who could stay married to a woman with ESP? *(The implication of this makes him*

uneasy; he picks up his drink and sips. MYRA *studies him)*
Well, don't fix me with that basilisk stare, whatever a basilisk happens to be. Wouldn't *you* like to
go into Sardi's again secure in the knowledge that
we're not going to be seated in the kitchen? . . . Do
you know how much this play could net its author
in today's market? Two million dollars, and that's
not including the *Deathtrap* T-shirts. If that's not a
reasonable motive for murder, I'd like to know
what is. I wish you hadn't told me about her . . .
(He picks up the phone and dials again) Ah, here we
go . . . Hello. Is this Clifford Anderson? . . . Sidney
Bruhl. *(Covers the phone and mouths "Not the stam-
merer" at* MYRA*)* . . . As a matter of fact I have. I
finished it about fifteen minutes ago, and I must
tell you in all sincerity that you've got an enormously promising first draft. I was just saying to
my wife Myra that if you give it the reshaping it
needs, point it up in the right places and work in
some laughs, it'll be right up there with *Sleuth* and
The Murder Game and *Dial "M."* It has the makings,
as we say . . . I should think you would be . . . Oh,
I know that feeling so well. I thought *The Murder
Game* was finished the first time 'round, and then
someone with much more experience in the theater took it in hand and revised it with me; im-
proved it tremendously, I don't mind admitting
. . . George S. Kaufman. He didn't take credit,
though God knows I urged him to, because he was
badly in debt at the time and didn't want it known

that he had a share of the royalties. But look, I could be quite wrong about this; what sort of reaction have you had from other people? . . . Oh? No one at all? *(Looks at* MYRA, *and away)* That's very flattering. But surely someone has read it: your friends, your wife, some of the twer—uh, people who were at the seminar? . . . Oh. I see. Hmm. That sounds ideal: complete isolation, and all you have to do is check the thermostat and water the plants. I'm surprised you've written only *one* play since July; I'd have tossed off three or four by now . . . *(*MYRA, *uneasy, has withdrawn a bit)* I am—a marvelous thriller. It's about a woman with ESP. Based on Helga ten Dorp; you know, the Dutch psychic? She's a neighbor of ours. *(Facing* MYRA*'s disapproval)* It's called *The Frowning Wife*, but that's only a working title; I'll have to come up with something jazzier than that. I love *Deathtrap*, incidentally—the title as well as the play. Or the promising first draft, I should say . . . Yes, I do. Far too many of them to give you over the phone. Perhaps we can get together sometime and go through the manuscript scene by scene. I'm free this evening, as a matter of fact; why don't you drive down? It's not very far . . . Oh. Hmm. Well, why don't you take the train down and I'll pick you up at the Westport station and run you over. It'll be better that way anyway. You'd have a devil of a time finding us; we're way off in the woods. Have to send up flares when we're expecting people . . . Do; I'll hold on. *(Covers the mouthpiece)* His car is in for repairs. He's house-sitting for a couple who are in Europe. Unmarried.

MYRA   Do you . . . think he'll be open to the idea of collaborating?

SIDNEY   *(Thinks—about several things)*   Yes, I think he might . . . Was George S. Kaufman still alive when *The Murder—(Uncovers the mouthpiece)* Yes? . . . That's a bit early; when's the next one? . . . That's too late; let's make it the seven-twenty-nine. *(Jotting it down)* And there's an eleven-oh-something from New York that I'm sure stops at Milford; you won't have any problem at all about getting back home. Would you bring the original with you? The carbon's a bit hard on these weary old eyes . . . Good. I'll see you at seven-twenty-nine then. Oh, Terence? Do you mind if I call you Terence? . . . Why? . . . Oh God, I'm sorry—Clifford! Clifford. I may be a few minutes late, Clifford; I have some errands to run. So just wait by the station and I'll be along eventually. In a navy-blue Mercedes . . . Right. Good-bye. *(He hangs up, sips his drink.* MYRA *is more than ever uneasy)* I *think* he's the one without obvious defects . . .

MYRA   What errands do you have to run?

SIDNEY   Didn't you say something about library books? Picking them up or dropping them off?

MYRA   No, I didn't.

SIDNEY   Oh. I thought you did. *(Considers his drink a moment, and looks at* MYRA *again)* The Xerox machine has been fixed, but he decided to wait a day or two longer in case I had any small suggestions to make. No one else has read it. No one even knows he's been working on it.

MYRA   And no one will see you picking him up . . .

SIDNEY   The thought did cross my mind. I'm so in the habit of planning crimes on paper . . .

MYRA   Why did you tell him to bring the original copy?

SIDNEY   You heard me. The carbon *is* a strain, and we *should* have two copies to go through. I don't want him leaning over my shoulder for two hours, exhaling cheeseburger.

MYRA   He probably has another carbon copy filed away somewhere.

SIDNEY   More than likely. And all his notes and outlines, early drafts . . . Opening night of my dazzling triumph his gray-haired mother comes down the aisle accompanied by the Milford and Westport police departments . . . *(The phone rings;* SIDNEY *takes it)* Hello? . . . How are you, Lottie? . . . No, I don't think so. I—have an idea I'm working on and I don't want to lose touch with it; it's in the embryo stage. But Myra might want to. Hold on a second. *(Covers the mouthpiece)* They're going to see the French thing at Fine Arts Two. *(*MYRA *shakes her head)* I could drop you off on the way . . .

MYRA   No. I don't want to see it, not tonight.

SIDNEY   Lottie? . . . Myra will pass too; she's a bit under the weather. Give us a report on it tomorrow, will you? Have fun. Good-bye. *(Hangs up)* You don't have to stand guard over me. I only kill when the moon is full.

MYRA   Why did you lie just now? Why didn't you tell her someone's coming to see you?

SIDNEY   Is it their business? *I* don't know why I lied; I'm just a liar.

MYRA   The moon was full last night, except for a sliver down near the bottom.

SIDNEY   Really? *(*MYRA *nods)* Well, I shall simply have to exercise massive self-control. And remind myself of that other carbon copy, which almost certainly exists.

MYRA   If not for that, Sidney—would you? Could you?

SIDNEY   Probably not. Probably I would chicken out. Even if he's the tiny one . . . They say that committing murder on paper siphons off the hostile impulses, and I'm sure it does. At the same time though, it opens one to the idea of committing real murder, gives it the familiar feel of a possibility worth considering—just as owning a weapon, and handling it . . . *(Takes an ornate dagger from its place)* opens one, however slightly, to the idea of using it. *(Toys with the dagger, hefts it)* But there's a world of difference between a paper victim and a real one. *(Replacing the dagger)* No, I'm sure Clifford Anderson will go home tonight in the same state of health in which he arrives, manuscript clutched in tiny or huge or relatively normal hand.

> *(MYRA goes to him and hugs him. He puts an arm around her, kisses her forehead)*

MYRA He'll jump at the chance to collaborate with you, and afterwards you'll do a play that's all your own.

SIDNEY I'm sure I shall, sooner or later.

MYRA Maybe you *could* do something based on Helga ten Dorp. But *not* called *The Frowning Wife*.

SIDNEY *The Smiling Wife*, a cheerful up kind of thriller. *(He gives* MYRA *another kiss and they separate)* You know, there could be an idea in *this*. A playwright who's . . . undergoing a dry period is sent a newly hatched play by a twerp who attended his seminar . . . *(MYRA has stopped by the door)* It's a possible opening, isn't it? If the play is obviously commercial and the playwright has a roomful of weapons?

MYRA Put it in your notebook.

16

SIDNEY   I will. *(Taps at the manuscript, frowns)* Pity he's
got the title *Deathtrap* . . .
(MYRA *stands uncertainly for a moment, then goes
out into the foyer and exits.* SIDNEY *stands tapping
at the manuscript, contemplating distasteful possibilities as the lights fade to darkness)*

SCENE TWO

As the lights come up, SIDNEY *has unlocked the front door from the outside and is showing* CLIFFORD ANDERSON *into the foyer, while* MYRA, *who has been fretting in the study, hurries to greet them. The draperies are drawn over the French doors, and all the room's lamps are lighted.* SIDNEY *has replaced his sweater with a jacket;* MYRA *has freshened up and changed into a simple dress.* CLIFFORD *is in his mid-twenties and free of obvious defects: an attractive young man in jeans, boots, and a heavy sweater. He carries a bulging Manila envelope.*

SIDNEY Actually it was built in seventeen-*ninety*-four, but they were out of nines at the hardware store, so I backdated it ten years.

CLIFFORD It's a beautiful house.

SIDNEY *(Closing the door)* Historical Society had kittens.

MYRA Hello!
(She offers her hand; CLIFFORD *shakes it warmly)*

SIDNEY This is Clifford Anderson, dear. My wife Myra.

CLIFFORD Hello. It's a pleasure to meet you.

MYRA Come in. I was be-   SIDNEY Watch out for
ginning to worry . . .   the beam.
(Ducking, CLIFFORD *comes into the study.* SIDNEY *follows)*

18

SIDNEY   You can always tell an authentic Colonial by the visitors' bruised foreheads. (MYRA *smiles nervously.* CLIFFORD *looks about, a bit awed*)

CLIFFORD   The room you work in?

SIDNEY   How did you guess.

CLIFFORD   The typewriter, and all these posters . . . (*He moves about, studying the window cards.* SIDNEY *watches him;* MYRA *glances at* SIDNEY. CLIFFORD *touches the Master's covered typewriter, then points at the wall*) Is that the mace that was used in *Murderer's Child?*

SIDNEY   Yes. And the dagger is from *The Murder Game.* (CLIFFORD *goes closer, touches the dagger blade*) Careful, it's sharp. The trick one was substituted in Act Two.

CLIFFORD   (*Moves his hand to an ax handle*)   *In for the Kill?*

SIDNEY   Yes.

CLIFFORD   I can't understand why that play didn't run . . .

SIDNEY   Critics peeing on it might be the answer. (CLIFFORD *goes on with his inspection*)

MYRA   The train must have been late. (SIDNEY *pays no notice*) Was it?

CLIFFORD   (*Turning*)   No, Mr. Bruhl was. The train was on time.

SIDNEY   I had to get gas, and Frank insisted on fondling the spark plugs.

(CLIFFORD *points at a window card)*

CLIFFORD   Do you know that *Gunpoint* was the first play I ever saw? I had an aunt in New York, and I came in on the train one Saturday—by myself, another first—from Hartford. She took me to the matinee. I was twelve years old.

SIDNEY   If you're trying to depress me, you've made it.

CLIFFORD   How? Oh. I'm sorry. But that's how I got hooked on thrillers.

SIDNEY   *Angel Street* did it to me. "Bella, where is that grocery bill? Eh? What have you done with it, you poor wretched creature?" I was fifteen.

MYRA   It sounds like a disease, being passed from generation to generation.

SIDNEY   It is a disease: *thrilleritis malignis,* the fevered pursuit of the one-set five-character moneymaker.

CLIFFORD   I'm not pursuing money. Not that I wouldn't like to have some, so I could have a place like this to work in; but that isn't the reason I wrote *Deathtrap.*

SIDNEY   You're still an early case.

CLIFFORD   It's *not* a disease, it's a tradition: a superbly challenging theatrical framework in which every possible variation seems to have been played. Can I conjure up a few new ones? Can I startle an audience that's *been* on Angel Street, that's dialed "M" for murder, that's witnessed the prosecution, ~~that's~~ played the murder game—

SIDNEY Lovely speech! And thanks for saving me for last.

CLIFFORD I was coming to *Sleuth.*

SIDNEY I'm glad I stopped you.

CLIFFORD So am I. I'm a little . . . euphoric about all that's happening.

SIDNEY As well you should be.

MYRA Would you like something to drink?

CLIFFORD Yes, please. Do you have some ginger ale?

MYRA Yes. Sidney? Scotch?

SIDNEY No, dear, I believe I'll have ginger ale too.
  (This gives MYRA *a moment's pause, after which she goes to the buffet)*

CLIFFORD These aren't *all* from your plays, are they?

SIDNEY God no, I haven't written *that* many. Friends give me things now, and I prowl the antique shops.

MYRA *There's* a disease.

SIDNEY *(Taking his keys out)* Yes, and a super excuse for not working. *(Indicating a pistol while en route to the desk)* I found this in Ridgefield just the other day —eighteenth-century German.

21

CLIFFORD   It's beautiful . . .

SIDNEY *(Unlocking the desk's center drawer)*   As you can see, I'm taking very good care of my "spiritual child." Lock and key . . .

CLIFFORD *(Unfastening his envelope)*   I've got the original.

SIDNEY *(Taking the manuscript from the drawer)*   Thank God. I should really be wearing glasses but my doctor told me the longer I can do without them, the better off I am. *(Offering the manuscript in the wrong direction)* Here you are. Oh, there you are.
> (CLIFFORD *smiles;* MYRA *turns to look and turns back to her ice and glasses.* CLIFFORD *takes a rubber-banded manuscript from the envelope)*

CLIFFORD   It's not in a binder. For the Xeroxing . . .

SIDNEY   Makes no never-mind.
> *(They exchange manuscripts)*

CLIFFORD   I've got the first draft here too. *(Sits near the desk)* There's a scene between Diane and Carlo in Act One that I may have been wrong to cut, and the Diane-and-Richard scene starts earlier, before they know Carlo is back.

SIDNEY *(Sitting behind the desk)*   Did you do several drafts?

CLIFFORD   Just the one. It's a mess, but I think you'll be able to decipher it, if you'd like to see those two scenes.

SIDNEY   I would. By all means. (CLIFFORD *extracts a less tidy manuscript from the envelope*) I had a feeling there was a Diane-and-Carlo scene I wasn't seeing . . . Before the murder?

CLIFFORD   Yes. I was afraid the act would run too long.
     (He hands the second manuscript over)

SIDNEY   Thanks. What else do you have in there?

CLIFFORD   Oh, the outline, which I departed from considerably. I made it the way you suggested, a page per scene, loose-leaf. And some lines I jotted down and never got to use.

SIDNEY   Threw away the ones you did use as you used them?

CLIFFORD   Yes.

SIDNEY   Same way I work . . .
     (MYRA comes over with glasses of ginger ale)

CLIFFORD   Everything was in the one envelope, so I just grabbed it. *(Taking a glass)* Thank you.

MYRA   You're welcome.
     (She gives SIDNEY his glass, along with an intent look)

SIDNEY   Thanks.

CLIFFORD   It's a two-hour walk to the station, so I had to leave right after we talked.
     (MYRA withdraws)

SIDNEY *Two hours?*

CLIFFORD I walk longer than that; I'm one writer who's not going to get flabby. I work out with weights every morning. I came *this close (Fingers slightly apart)* to making the Olympic decathlon team.

Do you Know [handwritten annotation]

SIDNEY Really?

CLIFFORD *(Hands wide apart)* Well, *this* close.

SIDNEY I'll be careful not to argue with you. I'm on the Olympic sloth team. Gold medal. Fall asleep in any position. *(Raises his glass, pretends to fall asleep and wake up)* Deathtrap.

CLIFFORD *Deathtrap.*

MYRA *Deathtrap. (*SIDNEY *turns.* MYRA *is now seated, glass in hand, needlework in her lap)* It'll be toasted with more than ginger ale someday, if Sidney is right about it, and I'm sure he is.

CLIFFORD I hope so. I toasted it with beer the other night.

MYRA We have some. Would you rather?

CLIFFORD No, no, this is fine, thanks.

SIDNEY *(To* MYRA*)* Are you planning to stay in here?

MYRA Yes.

CLIFFORD *(Manuscript open on his lap)* Do you think I overdid the set description? All the exact locations for each piece of furniture?

SIDNEY   The set description? *(Looking in the original manuscript)* I don't remember anything wrong with it . . . No, this is perfect, couldn't be better. *(Turns pages)* You certainly type beautifully . . . Electric?

CLIFFORD   No. I can't see electric typewriters; if there's a power failure you can't work.

SIDNEY   That's the whole point in owning one. *(Turning another page)* No, the real trouble with them, I find—with Zenobia here, at any rate—is that you can make only one decent carbon. The second carbon is so muddy as to be almost illegible. *(CLIFFORD turns a page. MYRA leans forward nervously)* You don't have that problem with—

MYRA *(Interrupting the question)*   Sidney has some wonderful ideas for improving the play, Mr. Anderson!

CLIFFORD   I'm—sure he does. I'm looking forward to hearing them.

SIDNEY   Couldn't you do that in the living room, dear?

MYRA   There's no good work light in there.

SIDNEY   I seem to recall a paisley chair with a light beside it bright enough for the engraving of Bibles on pinheads.

MYRA   It's *too* bright, and the chair is too low. I'll be quiet.

SIDNEY   Darling, this is Clifford's first play and I'm the first person to read it. I'm sure he'd prefer our discussion to be private. *(To* CLIFFORD*)* Wouldn't you? Don't be embarrassed to say so.

CLIFFORD   No, I don't mind Mrs. Bruhl being here. In fact, I like it. It makes me feel a little less as if I've been summoned to the principal's office.

SIDNEY   Oh. *(*MYRA *settles in)* I'm sorry if I awe you.

CLIFFORD   You do. All those plays, and the things you say . . . I never thought of calling my typewriter anything but Smith-Corona.

SIDNEY   As long as it answers . . .

CLIFFORD   *You're* welcome to read the play too, Mrs. Bruhl, if you'd like to.

MYRA   I would.

CLIFFORD   *(To* SIDNEY*)*   I'm curious to know how women are going to react to Diane's decision. About the gun.

MYRA·   Sidney told me a little about it at dinner, but he stopped at the surprises. I don't even know who kills whom.

CLIFFORD   Good. You shouldn't. *(To* SIDNEY*)*   I think that was the trouble with *Murderer's Child,* if you'll forgive me for saying so. From the opening curtain it was so obvious that Dr. Mannheim was going to bash poor Teddy. You didn't leave any room for doubt. I mean, the audience should suspect, yes, but they shouldn't be absolutely certain, should they? Doesn't that tend to diminish the suspense?

SIDNEY   Hmm . . . You may have a point there . . . I wish you had mentioned on the phone that you wanted Myra to read it. I'd have told you to bring another carbon, and she could be reading right now while we have our talk.

CLIFFORD   I didn't know she'd be interested, and anyway, I don't have one.
       (MYRA *is sitting forward again*)

SIDNEY   You don't have another carbon?

CLIFFORD   I only made the one. I thought I'd be Xeroxing the original as soon as I was through.

SIDNEY   Of course. There's no need for two or three any more in the age of Xerox.
       (*His eyes meet* MYRA's *and glance away.* CLIFFORD *gestures with his manuscript toward* MYRA)

CLIFFORD   She could read this one, and we could pass the pages back and forth. Or I could sit next to you.

SIDNEY   Wait. Let me think. I want to think for a moment.
       (SIDNEY *thinks—hard.* MYRA *tries to contain her growing anxiety but can't*)

MYRA   Mr. Anderson, Sidney is bursting with creative ideas about your play! I've never seen him so enthusiastic! He gets plays in the mail very often, finished plays that are ready for production supposedly—from his agent, from producers, from aspiring playwrights; and usually he just laughs and sneers and says the most disparaging things you could possibly imagine! I know he could improve your play tremendously! He could turn it into a hit that would run for years and years and make more than enough money for everyone concerned!

(She stops. CLIFFORD *stares.* SIDNEY *studies her)*

SIDNEY Is that what you meant by "I'll be quiet"?

MYRA *(Putting her needlework aside)* I *won't* be quiet. I'm going to say something that's been on my mind ever since your phone conversation. *(Rising, advancing on* CLIFFORD*)* It's very wrong of you to expect Sidney to give you the fruit of his years of experience, his hard-won knowledge, without any quid pro quo, as if the seminar were still in session!

CLIFFORD He *offered* to give me—

MYRA *(Turning on* SIDNEY*)* And it's very wrong of *you* to have offered to give it to him! *I* am the one in this household whose feet are on the ground, and whose eye is on the checkbook! Now, I'm going to make a suggestion to you, Sidney. It's going to come as a shock to you, but I want you to give it your grave and thoughtful and earnest consideration. Will you do that? Will you promise to do that for me? *(*SIDNEY, *staring, nods) Put aside the play you're working on.* Yes, put aside the play about Helga ten Dorp and how she *finds murderers,* and keys under clothes dryers; put it aside, Sidney, and help Mr. Anderson with *his* play. Collaborate with him. *That's* what I'm suggesting. *That's* what I think is the fair and sensible and *rational* thing to do in this situation. *Deathtrap,* by Clifford Anderson and Sidney Bruhl. Unless Mr. Anderson feels that, in deference to your age and reputation, it should be the other way around.

SIDNEY Hmm. That *is* a shocker. Put aside . . . *The Drowning Wife?*

CLIFFORD I thought it was "frowning."

SIDNEY *Frowning?* No. What kind of title would that be? *The Drowning Wife* is what I'm calling it, at the moment. It has these Women's Lib overtones, plus the ESP . . . *(Looking doubtfully at* MYRA*)* It's such a *timely* play . . .

MYRA *It will keep,* Sidney. People are always interested in psychics who can point at someone *(Points to him)* and say . . . *(Swings her finger to* CLIFFORD*)* "This man—murdered that man." *(Pointing at* SIDNEY *again. She lowers her hand)* Put it aside. Please. Do for Mr. Anderson . . . what George S. Kaufman did for you.

SIDNEY *(Gives her a look, then thinks)* That's awfully persuasive, Myra. *(To* CLIFFORD*)* How does it grab *you?*

CLIFFORD Oh wow. I suddenly feel as if I'm on the spot.

SIDNEY You are, really. Myra's put you there, put us both there.

29

MYRA I felt it should be brought up now, before—anything was done.

SIDNEY Yes, yes, you were quite right. Quite right. (CLIFFORD *is thinking*) What's your reaction, Clifford?

CLIFFORD *(Rises)* Well, first of all, I'm ~~overwhelmed~~, ~~really~~ honored ~~and staggered~~, that Sidney Bruhl would even *consider* the idea of putting aside one of his own plays to work with me on mine. I mean, there I was, sitting in that theater when I was twelve years old, and who would think that someday I'd be standing *here*, weighing the chance to—

SIDNEY *(Interrupting him)* We get the gist of this passage.

CLIFFORD It's a golden opportunity that I'm sure I ought to seize with both hands.

MYRA You should. Yes.

CLIFFORD But . . . the thing is . . . it's as if I went to a doctor, one of the world's leading specialists, and he recommended surgery. Well, even with my respect for his eminence and his experience, I would still want to get a second opinion, wouldn't I? I'm sure your ideas are terrific, but you're right, Mrs. Bruhl, it wouldn't be . . . fair for me to hear them now, without some sort of an understanding or arrangement. And to be perfectly honest, right now, *without* having heard them, I feel that *Deathtrap* is very good as it is. Not perfect, certainly; I guess it

could still use a little fine-tuning. But—I'm not
sure it needs surgery . . . What I ought to do, I
think, is Xerox a few copies tomorrow morning
and send them off to some of those agents you
recommended to us. If they say too that it needs
major rewriting, then I'll be coming back here
begging you to do what Mrs. Bruhl suggested, and
I'll be willing to make whatever arrangement you
think is right. The same one you had with Mr.
Kaufman, I guess . . . I hope I haven't offended
you.

SIDNEY   Not at all.

MYRA   Mr. Anderson, please. Agents know about
contracts; they don't know—

SIDNEY *(Interrupting her, gathering the two manuscripts together)*   Don't, Myra. Don't beg him. He'll think he
has the wealth of the Indies here, and we're Mr. and
Mrs. Jean Lafitte.

CLIFFORD   I'd never think anything like that, Mr.
Bruhl. I'm grateful that you're willing to go out of
your way to help me.

SIDNEY   But I'm not, really. Now that I've had a moment to consider the matter, I would never put aside
a play as timely and inventive as *The Drowning Wife*
to do wet-nurse work on one as speculative as *Deathtrap. (Hands the manuscripts over)* Sit down, Myra.
You're making me nervous, standing there hyper-
ventilating. *(*MYRA *withdraws a bit, warily)* Do as you

said—show it to a few agents. And if you decide that major rewrites *are* in order, get in touch. Who knows, I might hit a snag; it's happened once or twice.

CLIFFORD *(Fitting the two manuscripts into the envelope)* Thank you, I will.
　　(MYRA withdraws farther)

SIDNEY Though I doubt I shall; I have it completely outlined and I'm more than halfway done. And I have another play ready to go next, based on the life of Harry Houdini.

CLIFFORD Oh?

SIDNEY *(Rising)* Yes, magic is very in now. Look at the success of *The Magic Show.* Houdini's always been an idol of mine. *(Taking handcuffs from the wall)* These are a pair of his handcuffs . . .

MYRA *(On edge again)* Sidney . . .

SIDNEY Relax, darling; Clifford isn't the type of person who would steal someone else's idea. *(To CLIFFORD)* You wouldn't do that, would you?

CLIFFORD Of course not.

SIDNEY See? No cause for alarm. "His heart as far from fraud as heaven from earth." A remarkable man, Houdini. Made all his own magical apparatus, did you know that?

CLIFFORD No, I didn't.

SIDNEY   Magnificent craftsmanship. Have a look.
   (Tosses the open handcuffs to CLIFFORD*)*

MYRA   Sidney, *please!*

SIDNEY   *Sit down, Myra.*

MYRA   Don't! I beg you! For God's sake, *think!*

SIDNEY   He's an *honest young man!* Now, will you sit
   down and stop being so all-fired suspicious of everyone who comes through that door? *(To* CLIFFORD*)*
   We had a very nasty experience a few years back
   involving a plagiaristic playwright whose name I
   won't mention, since he's gone to his Maker, re-
   called for repairs. Ever since, Myra has gotten
   alarmed if I so much as tell a fellow writer the
   language I'm working in. Don't take it personally.
   Have a good look at those; they're quite remarkable.
      *(*MYRA *has turned away in anxiety.* SIDNEY *glances
      uneasily at her while* CLIFFORD, *who has rested his
      envelope and bound manuscript against the leg of his
      chair, examines the antique handcuffs.* MYRA *sits, fac-
      ing away from them)*

CLIFFORD   They look so old . . .

SIDNEY   They were made to. And apparently solid
   and escape-proof.

CLIFFORD   They certainly seem that way.

SIDNEY   Be my guest.

CLIFFORD   You mean put them on?

SIDNEY   Yes. That's what I mean when you're holding my prize pair of twelve-hundred-dollar Houdini handcuffs and I say, "Be my guest": "Put them on."

CLIFFORD   Twelve hundred dollars . . . Whew!
      (Impressed, he locks the handcuffs onto his wrists. MYRA *sits wincing)*

SIDNEY   Now turn your wrists like this, press, and pull. (CLIFFORD *follows the directions—and is still handcuffed)* You didn't do it right; it's got to be a single quick motion. Try again. (CLIFFORD *does; no dice)* Turn, press, pull; all in one.
      *(*CLIFFORD *makes several more tries)*

CLIFFORD   No, they're not opening.

SIDNEY   Hmm. They did for me yesterday morning; it's not a question of their not being oiled.

CLIFFORD *(Still   trying)*   I guess I'm just not Houdini . . .

SIDNEY   It's all right, I've got the key here. Somewhere. *(Begins rummaging nervously about the desktop)* Don't go on fussing with them; you're liable to ruin them.

CLIFFORD   Sorry.
      (He sits still. MYRA *turns around, slowly, fearfully.* CLIFFORD *smiles sheepishly at her; she tries to smile back.* SIDNEY *goes on searching)*

SIDNEY   Key, key, key, key. Where are you, little brass key?

(He begins looking in drawers. CLIFFORD *looks at his handcuffed wrists, and at* MYRA, *and at* SIDNEY, *and gets an idea)*

CLIFFORD   Do you know, this could be a good thriller! *(*SIDNEY *looks at him)* It could! I mean it!

SIDNEY   How so?

CLIFFORD   Well . . . a young playwright sends his first play to an older playwright ~~who conducted a seminar that the young playwright attended~~. Nobody else has read it, and then he comes to *visit* the older playwright, *to get some ideas for rewrites,* and he brings along the original and all his notes and everything. Of course, you'd have to have the Xerox breaking down, to explain why there are only the two copies, and the play would have to be a very good one—the one the young playwright wrote, I mean—and the older playwright would have to have nothing much going for him at the time . . .

SIDNEY   An enormous concatenation of unlikely circumstances, don't you think?

CLIFFORD   Yes, maybe . . . But we've almost got it here, haven't we? The only difference is that you've got *The Drowning Wife* and the Houdini play, and *Deathtrap* probably isn't worth killing for . . . I'll bet nobody even saw me getting into your car . . .

SIDNEY   Well, there you are: You've licked the second-play problem.
   (He resumes searching)

35

CLIFFORD I think it could be turned into something fairly interesting . . . What do you think, Mrs. Bruhl?

MYRA I—don't like it. It frightens me.

SIDNEY *(Turning to the weapons on the wall)* I wonder if I could have put it up here somewhere.
> *(CLIFFORD looks curiously at MYRA, and at SIDNEY nervously touching the various weapons, and at his handcuffed wrists. He thinks a bit. And a bit more. And a lot more. He thinks very hard)*

CLIFFORD Oh, I forgot to mention—I should be getting a phone call any minute now. *(SIDNEY turns and looks at him)* There's a girl who's coming to see me at eight-thirty—that's around what it is now, isn't it?—and I couldn't reach her before I left, so I left a note on the hall mirror telling her where I am and giving the number *(Rising and backing away)* so she can call and find out what train I'll be taking back. So she can pick me up at the station. One two-hour walk per day is just about enough for me. *(Turns and smiles)* So I hope you find the key soon, or else you're going to have to hold the phone for me.

SIDNEY *(Stands looking at him for a moment)* How is she going to get in to *read* the note?

CLIFFORD She has a key.

SIDNEY You're not a very conscientious house-sitter.

CLIFFORD She's honest.

SIDNEY You said in the car that you don't know any-one in Milford except a few tradespeople.

CLIFFORD She's from Hartford. Her name is Marietta Klenofski and she teaches at Quirk Middle School. Phys Ed.

SIDNEY Where did you get the number? It's not listed.

CLIFFORD They gave it to me at the university, along with your address. I'm friendly with Mrs. Beecham there.

SIDNEY Beecham?

CLIFFORD The short red-haired lady. With the eye-shade.

SIDNEY I hope she gave you the right number. I had it changed a few weeks ago—an obscene caller was boring us—and I don't think I notified old U. of Conn. What number did you leave for Ms. Klenof-ski?

CLIFFORD I don't remember it.

SIDNEY Two-two-six, three-oh-four-nine? Or two-two-six, five-four-five-seven?

CLIFFORD The first one. Three-oh-four-nine.

SIDNEY The new number. Hmm. I must have notified the university and clean forgot about it. How strange, and how untypical of me.

CLIFFORD Would you go on looking for the key, please?

SIDNEY Certainly.
(*Turns, considers, reaches to the wall*)

MYRA *My heart won't take it!*

SIDNEY (*Plucking something from a ledge*) Won't take
what, dear? (*Turning, showing a key*) My finding the
key? (*Looks at* MYRA, *and at* CLIFFORD) I do believe the
two of you thought I was going to grab the mace and
do a Dr. Mannheim . . . Clifford? Is that why you've
withdrawn so far upstage?

CLIFFORD (*Shrugs uncomfortably, points toward his chair*)
You can't write a play like that and not have a mind
that . . . envisions possibilities.

SIDNEY True, very true. I'm slightly paranoid myself.
(*Coming around the desk*) What's *your* excuse, oh loyal
and trusting wife? (MYRA *looks at him—as he puts the
key on a table by* CLIFFORD'*s chair—and turns away*)
Eleven years of marriage and she thinks I'm capable
of a flesh-and-blood murder. There's a lesson for
you in that, Clifford. Come uncuff yourself. *Deathtrap* is promising, but it's not *that* promising.
(*He moves back around the desk*)

CLIFFORD (*Going toward the chair*) I'm glad it isn't.

SIDNEY No, I think your best invention so far is the
name "Marietta Klenofski." That's lovely. I con-
gratulate you.

CLIFFORD Thanks.
(*Sitting in the chair, he picks up the key and leans his
hands into the lamplight*)

SIDNEY   I can see the sweat on her forearms after the basketball game . . . Mrs. Beecham's eyeshade, I thought, was a bit much.

CLIFFORD   I thought it was the kind of convincing detail you told us to try for. Are you sure this is the right key?

SIDNEY   *(Coming around to him)* Ye gods, Houdini opened them inside a milk can under ten feet of water; do you mean to say you can't do it in—
   (He whips a garrotte around CLIFFORD'*s throat, and pulling at its two handles, hauls him upward from the chair.* CLIFFORD, *choking, tries to get his fingers under the wire but can't.* MYRA *whirls, screaming)*

MYRA   *My God, Sidney! Stop! Stop it!*

SIDNEY   *Stay back! Stay away!*

MYRA   *Oh my God! My God!*
   *(*CLIFFORD *has thrust his manacled hands back over his head, trying to find* SIDNEY'*s head, while* SIDNEY, *grimly determined, strains at the garrotte handles. The chair tumbles.* MYRA *turns away, her hands over her face, moaning and crying.* SIDNEY *hauls* CLIFFORD *about by the garrotte, evading his groping hands, his kicking legs. A lamp falls.* CLIFFORD *catches one of* SIDNEY'*s hands and wrenches at it. Blood trickles down* CLIFFORD'*s wire-bound throat.* MYRA *turns and looks and turns away again, never stopping her moaning and lamentation.* CLIFFORD, *pop-eyed and hawking, falls forward before the fire-*

39

place, his shackled arms outflung; SIDNEY *goes down with him and kneels astride him, keeping his fierce hold on the handles. When* CLIFFORD *is finally and surely dead,* SIDNEY *relaxes his grip, lets go, sits for a moment on* CLIFFORD*'s back, then reaches forward and feels at a wrist within its handcuff.* MYRA *sits, weeping, moaning.* SIDNEY *gets up, breathing hard, trembling a little. He gets out his handkerchief, wipes his hands and his face, looks at* MYRA. *He rights the chair, picks up the lamp, puts it in its place and straightens its shade—not very successfully because his hands are shaking badly now. He clasps them a moment, then turns to the desk, picks up a key, and crouching beside* CLIFFORD, *unlocks and removes the handcuffs. He rises, wiping the cuffs with the handkerchief, and goes and replaces them on the wall, then returns to* CLIFFORD*'s body.* MYRA *is staring at him)*

SIDNEY   Right on the rug. One point for neatness. *(He crouches again and unwinds the garrotte from* CLIF-FORD*'s throat, then turns the ends of the hearthrug over* CLIFFORD*'s body. Rising, he wipes the garrotte with the handkerchief, and meets* MYRA*'s wondering stare)* Your heart seems to have taken it.

MYRA *(Keeps staring at him awhile)*   Barely.

SIDNEY *(Looks away, wiping at the garrotte)*   We'll give it a rest on the Riviera, after the opening. And we'll have a housekeeper again, so you can take things easy. Another car too, a goddamn Rolls.

(Looks at the blood-streaked handkerchief, wipes the garrotte some more)

MYRA   We're going to be in prison!

SIDNEY *(Throws the handkerchief into the fireplace and crosses the room)*   A young would-be playwright walks away from his house-sitting job. The police won't even bother to yawn.
(He puts the garrotte in its place)

MYRA   Leaving his clothes? And his typewriter?

SIDNEY   Why not? Who can figure these young people nowadays? Especially the would-be writers. Maybe he realized he *wouldn't* be—*(Picking up the envelope and the bound manuscript)*—and went off to preach ecology. *(Going back behind the desk)* Or to join the Reverend Sun Myung Moon. *(Puts the envelope and manuscript down, opens the manuscript)* Who knows? The place might be broken into, and poor little Smith-Corona stolen.
(He tears out the first page and puts it aside; unfastens the envelope and takes out the two unbound manuscripts; removes their first pages)

MYRA   What are you—going to do with him?

SIDNEY *(Examining other papers that were in the envelope)* Bury him. Behind the garage. No, in the vegetable patch—easier digging. *(He examines the last scraps of paper and puts them down; opens the desk's center drawer and puts the three manuscripts into it; closes and locks it. MYRA puts her face into her hands, overcome by grief and*

41

shock again. SIDNEY *gathers the papers and loose pages, the envelope, the letter that came with the play)* Take a brandy or something. *(He goes to the fireplace, and crouching by* CLIFFORD*'s body, tosses everything in; takes a match from a holder, strikes it, and sets the papers afire. He tosses the match in, rises, watches, then moves away and faces* MYRA, *who is studying him)* I'm going to be a winner again! All our dear friends are going to see *you* living on *my* money! Picture their confusion. *(*MYRA *looks into her lap.* SIDNEY *goes and throws open the draperies, unbolts and opens the French doors. He looks toward the treetops)* Full moon, all right. *(He comes back to the hearth, and crouching, rearranges* CLIFFORD*'s body for carrying)* I hope this isn't going to become a monthly practice. *(He straightens up, takes his jacket off and puts it on a chair, rubs his hands and readies himself; meets* MYRA*'s gaze)* Would you mind helping me carry him? *(*MYRA *looks at him for a moment, and looks away)* It's been *done*, Myra. I don't see the point in my getting a hernia. *(*MYRA *looks at him again, and after a moment, rises and comes over. The lights begin dimming as* SIDNEY *lifts* CLIFFORD*'s rug-wrapped shoulders.* MYRA *lifts his feet. They heft him up between them and carry him toward the French doors,* SIDNEY *going backwards)* Thank God he wasn't the fat one.

(The lights fade to darkness)

When the lights come up, MYRA *is sitting and thinking, an empty brandy glass in her hand. The moonlight outside the French doors is stronger now and coming from directly overhead.*

MYRA *looks at her glass, and after a moment, rises, goes to the buffet, and pours herself a small amount of brandy.* SIDNEY *comes to the French doors, wipes his feet, brushes dirt from his trouser legs, and enters. He looks at* MYRA—*who has turned and is looking at him*—*and enters, closes the doors, and pulls the draperies over them. He comes farther into the room.*

SIDNEY   Make mine a double. I've got myself a bit of a chill. *(Takes the breast-pocket handkerchief from his jacket on the chair; wipes his hands)* Along with incipient blisters, aching arms, and small devils poking pitchforks into what I believe is my lumbago. *(Picks up the jacket, puts it on)* In *Murderer's Child* I had Dr. Mannheim bury Teddy in forty-five minutes. In future I'll know better. *(*MYRA *goes and resumes her seat while* SIDNEY *puts the handkerchief back in his breast pocket and picks up the wrong handcuff key from the floor)* We're out one hearthrug, but I saw some nice ones in the Yield House the other day. *(He pockets the key, puts the chair in its exact place; sees* MYRA *sitting and no sign of his brandy. He considers this, then picks up the ginger-ale glasses and heads for the buffet)* I have a feeling you're about to deliver a speech. Would you

43

mind holding off until I've poured my own brandy and sat down?

MYRA   I had intended to. I've learned *something* in eleven years of melodrama.

SIDNEY   Good girl. *(Pours his brandy and crosses with it, groaning and rubbing the small of his back; sits, painfully, sips the brandy, and stretches out a bit more comfortably)* Go.

MYRA *(Waits a moment, and does)*   I'd be very happy living on your money, but I don't relish the thought of living on his. I've tried to understand how you could do it, bearing in mind your disappointments and your . . . embarrassment in our financial situation, but I can't. And how will you be able to feel like a winner when we'll both know it's his play? I can't understand that either. You're . . . alien to me, Sidney, and it can't be only since five o'clock this afternoon. You must always have been very different from the person I thought you were. *(*SIDNEY *is troubled by the speech)* I don't think the police are going to be as unconcerned as you do, so I don't want anything to happen that will look suspicious if they come to question us, but—

SIDNEY *(Interrupting her)*   How will they? He vanished from Milford; this is Westport.

MYRA   They'll check into his past associations! He must have gotten your address from the university, even if he did lie about the phone number!

SIDNEY If they come I'll simply say he wrote to me. A twerpy little letter asking for advice. And I answered it. Or maybe I just threw it away.

MYRA *(Rises, goes to the buffet, puts her glass down and turns)* In a month or so, if we haven't been arrested, I want you to leave. We'll have a few arguments in people's living rooms—you can write them for us, little tiffs about money or something—and then you'll move out. I wish you could take the vegetable patch with you, but since you can't, you'll buy it from me, as soon as the money starts rolling in. Before the Rolls-Royce and before you go to the Riviera! *(*SIDNEY, *concerned, rises and starts toward her; she's growing more distraught)* You'll buy the vegetable patch, and the house, and the whole nine-point-three acres! We'll get Buck Raymond or Maury Escher to set a fair price!

> *(She turns and moves away, near tears, as* SIDNEY *reaches for her)*

SIDNEY Darling, you've had a shocking and—

MYRA Get away from me!

SIDNEY You've had a shocking and painful experience and so have I. I'm terrified that I'll be caught and absolutely guilt-ridden about having been insane enough to do it. I'm going to give half the money to the New Dramatists League, I swear I am! . . . This isn't the time to talk about *anything*. In a few days, when we're both ourselves again, things will look much cheerier.

45

MYRA   You *are* yourself, right now. And so am I. In a few days— *(The doorbell chime stops her.* SIDNEY *freezes.* MYRA *points toward the door)* Go ahead. "He wrote me a twerpy letter, Officer."

SIDNEY   It must be Lottie and Ralph, come to yammer about the movie . . .

MYRA *(Wiping her cheeks)*   It's probably Helga ten Dorp.

SIDNEY   Don't be silly. *(The doorbell chimes again)* It's Lottie and Ralph, damn them. We've got to let them in. Can you face them? Maybe you'd better go upstairs. I'll tell them you—

MYRA *(Interrupting him)*   No. I'll stay here, and let you worry that I'll fall apart! *(*SIDNEY *eyes her anxiously. The doorbell chimes a third time.* SIDNEY *starts for the door)*

SIDNEY   Coming! *(*MYRA *tries to compose herself; moves into view of the door)* Who is it?

VOICE *(Offstage)*   I am your neighbor in house of McBains. Please, will you let me come in? *(*SIDNEY *turns, wide-eyed.* MYRA *too is startled and frightened)* Is most urgent I speak to you. I call the information but the lady will tell me not your number. Please, will you let me come in? *(*SIDNEY *turns to the door)* I am friend of Paul Wyman. Is most urgent!

SIDNEY *(Opening the door)*   Come in.
        *(*HELGA TEN DORP *comes into the foyer, a stocky strong-jawed Teutonic woman in her early fifties, in*

*the throes of considerable distress. She wears slacks and
a hastily seized and unfastened jacket)*

HELGA   I apologize for so late I come, but you will
forgive when I make the explaining. *(She comes into
the study.* SIDNEY *closes the door) Ja, ja,* is room I see.
Beams, and window like so . . . *(Holds her forehead,
wincing)* And the pain! Such pain! *(Sees* MYRA *and
recognizes her as the source of it; approaches her)* Pain.
Pain. Pain. Pain. *(Moves her hands about* MYRA, *as if
wanting to touch and comfort her but unable to)* Pain.
Pain. Pain!

SIDNEY   *(Coming nervously toward her)*   We're neither of
us up to snuff today . . .

HELGA   *(Turns, sees the weapons)   Ei!* Just as I see them!
Uuuch! Why keep you such pain-covered things?

SIDNEY   They're antiques, and souvenirs from plays.
I'm a playwright.

HELGA   *Ja,* Sidney Bruhl; Paul Wyman tells me. We
make together book.

SIDNEY   My wife Myra . . .

MYRA   How do you do . . .

HELGA   What gives you such pain, dear lady?

MYRA   Nothing. I'm—fine, really.

HELGA   No, no; something you see pains you. *(To both
of them)* Paul tells you of *me?* I am Helga ten Dorp.
I am psychic.

47

SIDNEY   Yes, he did. In fact, we were going to ask—

HELGA *(Interrupting him)*   For hours now I feel the pain from here. And more than pain. Since eight-thirty, when begins *The Merv Griffin Show.* I am on it next week; you will watch?

SIDNEY   Yes, yes, certainly. Make a note of that, Myra.

HELGA   ~~Thursday night. Peter Hurkos also. What they want *him* for, I do not know.~~ I call the Information but the lady will tell me not your number. I call Paul but he is not at home; he is in place with red walls, eating with chopsticks. I call the Information again. I say, "Is urgent, you *must* tell me number; I am Helga ten Dorp. I am psychic." She say, "*Guess* number." I try, but only I see the two-two-six, which is everybody, *ja?* So I come here now. *(Looking sympathetically at* MYRA*)* Because pain gets worse. And more than pain . . .

> *(She moves away and wanders the room, a hand to her forehead.* SIDNEY *and* MYRA *look anxiously at each other)*

MYRA   More than pain?

HELGA   *Ja,* is something else here, something frightening. No, it will interfere.

SIDNEY   What will?

HELGA   The drink you would give me. Must keep unclouded the head. Never drink. Only when images become too many. Then I get drunk. *(She goes close to the weapons, one hand to her forehead, the other hand passing back and forth.* SIDNEY *and* MYRA *stand motionless as* HELGA*'s hand passes over the garrotte. She takes up the dagger, turns with it, closes her eyes)* Was used many times by beautiful dark-haired woman. But only pretending—

SIDNEY   That's amazing! It's from my play *The Murder Game* and it was used every night by a beautiful dark-haired actress!

HELGA   Will be used again. By another woman. Not in play. But . . . *because* of play . . . *(Opens her eyes)* Because of play, another woman uses this knife. *(*SIDNEY *and* MYRA *stare at her. She replaces the dagger)* You should put away these things.

SIDNEY   Yes, yes, I think I will. In a month or so I'll sell the whole collection. Tired of them anyway.

HELGA   May be too late. *(Looks gravely at* SIDNEY *and* MYRA*)* I do not enjoy to make-unhappy people, but I must speak when I see something, *ja?*

SIDNEY   Well, I don't know actually; you *could* keep quiet. I mean, you're supposed to be resting, aren't you? Not in your own country—

HELGA   Must speak. Is why God gives gift. Is danger here. Much danger. *(To* SIDNEY*)* To you. *(To* MYRA*)* And to you. Is—death in this room. Is something that—invites death, that carries death . . . Deathtrap? This is word in English, "deathtrap"?

MYRA   Yes . . .

49

SIDNEY It's the title of a play I've been working on. That's where you've got it from. There's a death in the play; I'm sure that's what you're . . . responding to. I've been working there at the desk.

HELGA *(Moving around the desk, touching it)* Maybe . . . But feels like *real* death.

SIDNEY I try to be convincing, act everything out as I write it.
> *(*HELGA*'s attention is caught by the chair in which* CLIFFORD *sat. She goes to it, hesitates, takes hold of its back with both hands, closes her eyes, throws back her head.* MYRA *trembles;* SIDNEY *puts a hand to her shoulder)*

HELGA Man . . . in boots . . . Young man . . . *(Opens her eyes, looks at* SIDNEY*)* Here in this room—he attacks you.

SIDNEY He—attacks me?

HELGA *(Indicating the weapons)* With one of those. Comes as friend. To help you? To work with you? But attacks. *(Closes her eyes, shakes her head)* Is confusion here . . .

SIDNEY Yes, well, I'll certainly be on the lookout for a young man in boots! We're going to be Japanese from now on—shoes off at the door!

HELGA He sits in this chair . . . and he talks of . . . Diane . . .

SIDNEY There's a Diane in the play.

HELGA   And two other people . . . Smith—and Colonna. No, one person. Small. Black. *(Opens her eyes)* Is in play a black man, Smith Colonna?

SIDNEY   Never heard the name before.

HELGA   *(Closes her eyes again)*   Is very confusing image. *(Shakes her head, opens her eyes)* Is gone now. Nothing else comes.

SIDNEY   Well, that was a most impressive demonstration! Wasn't it, dear? *(To HELGA, who is coming away from the chair, collecting herself)* The way you picked up the name of the play, and Diane, and the dagger business—really awesome!

HELGA   Remember what else I tell you. Dagger is used again, by woman, because of play. And man in boots attacks you. Of these two things I am certain. All else is—confusing. *(To MYRA)* Pain is less now, *ja?*

MYRA   Yes. There wasn't any, really.
    (She smiles nervously at her)

SIDNEY   What a marvelous gift! I must confess I've been skeptical about ESP, but you've convinced me it's genuine.

HELGA   Oh yes, is genuine, and sometime not happy gift to be owner of.

MYRA   Have you always had it?

HELGA   Since I was child. Never could I enjoy a game of hide-and-go-seek. Was too easy, you understand? And parents did not wrap Christmas presents—

why wasting paper? Later, in my teen ages, walking with boys—*ach*, such images!

SIDNEY   Won't you have that drink now? I'd like very much to talk with you.

HELGA   No, thank you. I must go back to house. You will come take dinner with me sometime. I will tell you all of my life. Would make very good play. *(To* MYRA*)* When child you are living in large house with yellow shutters, *ja?*

MYRA   That's right! Yes!

HELGA *(Nods complacently)*   Always when moon is full I am in top form. *(Shakes* MYRA*'s hand)* Good night.

MYRA   Good night.

HELGA *(Her face clouds; she touches* MYRA*'s cheek)*   Be careful. *(She releases* MYRA*'s hand and turns and takes* SIDNEY*'s, which he gives a shade uneasily)* You also . . .

SIDNEY   I intend to. No boots allowed. Good night.

HELGA   Good night. *(She turns and starts toward the foyer,* SIDNEY *following.* HELGA *stops, turns, points warningly at* SIDNEY *and at* MYRA*)* Remember. Thursday night—*Merv Griffin Show.*
    (She turns and goes out the front door. SIDNEY *closes and bolts it, then comes back into the study)*

SIDNEY   Well! If that's the best she can do, there's nothing to worry about.

MYRA   You're not afraid of the danger she saw?

SIDNEY   Not especially.

MYRA   We're going to be arrested!

SIDNEY   I don't see how. If the police *do* come by, and *do* bring her into it—which hardly seems likely— well, what of it? She'll have them combing the tristate area for a small black boy with two spools of ribbon. *(Indicating his ears)* One here, one here, going through his mouth.

MYRA   She saw him sitting there! She heard him speaking!

SIDNEY   But she had the main point backwards! *(Takes MYRA's shoulders)* You'll see; there's nothing to worry about. I'll boil that thing *(Pointing to the garrotte)* tomorrow morning, or throw it in the garbage, and that'll be the end of it. In a week or so it'll all be behind us. *(MYRA turns away, moves from his hands)* I couldn't help myself, Myra. I saw that play going out into the world tomorrow morning, and him sitting there so young, so lucky . . . Don't decide yet about kicking the old boy out. And please, I beg you, don't entertain thoughts of using the dagger. *(MYRA turns, shocked)* Just a joke. That was another of her confused images, I'm sure. Though if we do get a housekeeper, I'll want her to have terrifically good references.

MYRA   Sell the collection.

SIDNEY   Probably I should. *(Turning to look at it, moving closer)* I will. Not right away, though; it would look too suspicious. *(Picks up the dagger, toys with it)* Amazing, isn't it? Eighteen years, and Tanya's aura still permeates it.

MYRA   Put it away somewhere.

SIDNEY *(Shrugs, opens a desk drawer and puts the dagger into it, closes it)*   Exit dagger, into desk.
   (He switches the desk lamp off)

MYRA   Part of me—was hoping you would do it. *(Nods)* At the same time that I was terrified you would, part of me was hoping. I saw the money too. And your name . . .
   (SIDNEY goes to her, takes her in his arms; she stands passively)

SIDNEY   You tried to stop me, you did your best. It was my doing and mine only. You helped me carry him because I asked you to, and you were too stunned and too . . . in the habit of helping me to refuse. If anything should go wrong, there must never be any confusion whatsoever on that point. *(He raises her chin and kisses her on the lips; she begins to respond to the kiss)* But nothing *will* go wrong. In a few weeks we'll be celebrating. "Leading Producer Options New Sidney Bruhl Thriller. Successful Playwrights Admit Envy." *(*MYRA *tries to smile.* SIDNEY *gives her a brief second kiss)* Let's lock up and turn in. *(He goes to turn a lamp off.* MYRA *hesitates, then turns another lamp off)* Is it possible that murder is an aphrodisiac? What

a blow that would be to importers of ginseng
root, not to mention the Department of Health,
Education, and— *EEEAH!*

*(He has cried out because he has put his hand between
the draperies to check the doorbolt, and the hand has
been seized by* CLIFFORD, *who, covered with dirt,
comes through the draperies trying to brain* SIDNEY
with a length of firewood. MYRA *cowers, dumbstruck
and paralyzed with terror. In the light from the foyer
and the one lamp still lit,* CLIFFORD's *bloody throat
can be seen as he wields the firewood.* SIDNEY *tries to
parry it with his free arm, but* CLIFFORD *wrenches the
captive hand up behind* SIDNEY's *back and forces him
to the desk and down onto it.* CLIFFORD *beats and
smashes at* SIDNEY's *head, each blow audible, till* SID-
NEY *lies still.* MYRA *moans and gibbers, biting at her
fingers.* CLIFFORD *prods* SIDNEY *a few times, then
stands straight, draws a deep breath, and turns. Raising the length of firewood, he advances on* MYRA)

MYRA   No. No. Please. He couldn't help himself. *(She
retreats around the side of a chair as* CLIFFORD *comes
closer, raises the firewood higher)* I tried to stop—
*(Her left arm shoots out straight as she falls against
the side of the chair, gasping, clutching her chest. She
hangs frozen over the chair arm for a moment—while*
CLIFFORD *stands over her ready to swing—and then
her eyes glaze and she slips back down slowly to the
floor.* CLIFFORD *is wary, uncertain. He looks down at
her, then crouches, the firewood still upraised. With his*

55

left hand he checks her partly concealed body, holding her wrist, moving her head from side to side, touching her throat. He lowers the firewood and stands up straight; looks down at her for a moment, breathing deeply)

CLIFFORD   She's dead . . . I'm positive. *(SIDNEY bestirs himself and gets up from the desk. Rubbing himself and straightening his jacket, he comes and stands by CLIFFORD; they look down at MYRA)* It worked . . .

SIDNEY   How could it not? She's had minor ones over much less. *(He looks down sadly at MYRA's body. CLIFFORD looks sympathetically at him and withdraws a few steps and turns away. Tucking the lightweight length of imitation firewood under his arm, he takes out a handkerchief and wipes some of the dirt from his face, the fake blood from his throat. SIDNEY breathes a sigh over MYRA, and rubbing the back of his head, comes and joins CLIFFORD)* I've got news for you: Styrofoam hurts. *(CLIFFORD shrugs apologetically)* You used it a hell of a lot harder than you did in the motel.

CLIFFORD   The added adrenalin of the actual performance. *(SIDNEY takes the firewood from under CLIFFORD's arm and goes with it toward the French doors)* You didn't make the strangling a jolly experience. *(SIDNEY opens the draperies all the way and steps outside; he comes back minus the firewood and plus the rolled-up hearthrug; closes the doors and bolts them)* How about that Helga ten Dorp? I almost had a heart attack myself out there.

SIDNEY *(Closing the draperies)* Same here.
(He turns a lamp on, and unrolls the hearthrug before the fireplace. CLIFFORD *is wiping his hands)*

CLIFFORD Spooky, the way she saw I was going to attack you.

SIDNEY *(Placing the rug properly)* She was a little off-base, though. She had you doing it with one of the weapons.

CLIFFORD That must have been the garrotte getting mixed in.

SIDNEY "*Ja.* Is very confusing image." *(Done with the rug, he turns and exchanges a smile with* CLIFFORD*)* Side of your nose. *(He touches his own nose;* CLIFFORD *wipes his.* SIDNEY *heads for the desk)* It's just as well she came. Now she'll be telling everyone she felt the physical pain of the oncoming heart attack. *(Turns the desk lamp on)* Every little bit helps. I've been telling people for days that Myra was under the weather. *(Straightening the disarray)* Not that any supporting evidence is needed, really.

CLIFFORD *(Pocketing the handkerchief)* I'd better get my things in.

SIDNEY *(Opening a bottom drawer)* No rush. I'm not going to call the doctor for a few minutes yet. We don't want them working any miracles of resuscitation, do we?

CLIFFORD What if Madam ten Dorp comes back?

SIDNEY *(Replacing the garrotte on the wall with one similar to it)* I can't think why she should. The pain has stopped, hasn't it?

CLIFFORD Yes. I hadn't thought of that.

SIDNEY *(Putting the garrotte from the wall into the drawer)* Don't move around too much; you're shedding dirt. *(Opens another drawer, takes out the dagger)* I'll bet you were glad to hear my "Exit dagger" line.

CLIFFORD Was that for my benefit?

SIDNEY *(Putting the dagger in its place)* Of course. I was going to suggest putting it away myself if she didn't. I was afraid the prediction might have made you uneasy. *(Unlocking the center drawer)* I had visions of you haring off into the woods, leaving me with a live wife, an imaginary corpse *(Taking out the manuscripts)* and no sure-fire can't-miss thriller to justify the one to the other.

CLIFFORD I'd never have done that.

SIDNEY *(Heading for the fireplace with the manuscripts)* Well, I just thought I'd relieve any possible anxiety. *(Stops)* I don't think I'd better burn these now. It'll take too long.

CLIFFORD Why burn them at all? They're just old manuscripts.

SIDNEY True. We could cut them up and use the backs for scrap. That's so chintzy, though. Oh, what

the hell. *(Throws the manuscripts in the fireplace, crouches, takes a match)* I'll say I was cleaning out my files when the Grim Reaper struck.
(He strikes the match)

CLIFFORD   The closer you can stay to the truth, the better off you are.

SIDNEY *(Lighting a corner)*   You're a fount of homey wisdom, Cliffy-boy. *(Lights another corner)* Farewell, *Deathtrap*. Would that you were the genuine article.

CLIFFORD   We can put my desk right here.

SIDNEY *(Tossing the match in, rising and turning)*   No, I have a surprise for you.

CLIFFORD   Let me guess. I work in the maid's room.

SIDNEY   Would I do that to you? You're working right here in the handsomely converted stable, as promised.

CLIFFORD   Then what's the surprise?

SIDNEY   You'll see, after the obsequies. *(Moving to the front of the desk)* I hope you won't mind Zenobia tearing along at full speed. I really am going to try something on ESP. That was an awfully impressive demonstration she gave, despite the mistakes.

CLIFFORD   I'm ready to get to work too.

SIDNEY   The thing you mentioned at the seminar?

CLIFFORD   No, I've got a better idea . . . Last week, while I was cleaning out my desk, I suddenly realized that there's a play *there*, in a typical urban welfare office.

SIDNEY   A thriller?

CLIFFORD   No. The truth is, I've begun to lose interest in thrillers. I want to try something . . . more honest, more relevant.

SIDNEY *(Reaching into his pocket)*   Even though you used those words, I'm going to let you stay here. *(Giving his car keys to* CLIFFORD*)* Go get your things; I'll call the doctor now.

CLIFFORD   Right.
   (He starts for the front door. SIDNEY *dials the phone while* CLIFFORD *tries the door, unbolts it, and goes out, leaving the door open.* SIDNEY *sits on the edge of the desk, the phone at his ear. He looks toward* MYRA'S *body and grows suitably sober)*

SIDNEY   Is he there? . . . Sidney Bruhl, B-r-u-h-l. Would you have him call me right away, please? It's urgent . . . My wife's had a heart attack . . . I'm afraid there's no use in that . . . Two-two-six, three-oh-four-nine.
   (He hangs up, sighs. CLIFFORD *comes through the front door with two garment bags, a tennis racket, and a large plaid suitcase. He knees the door closed and comes to the doorway, puts down the suitcase and racket)*

CLIFFORD I left the weights for tomorrow. And the typewriter.
    (He tosses the keys)

SIDNEY *(Catching them)* Ah yes, little Mr. Colonna.

CLIFFORD That was funny, wasn't it? *(Sidney nods, pocketing the keys)* On his way?

SIDNEY Answering service.

CLIFFORD Wouldn't you know. *(Picks up the suitcase and racket)* Well, see you later. How long do you think it'll be?

SIDNEY A couple of hours at least. I may have to—go with her; I don't know.

CLIFFORD Mmm. Well, *ciao*.

SIDNEY *Ciao.* (CLIFFORD *moves away*) Oh, Cliff? (CLIFFORD *comes back*) The floor up there creaks badly. So do a quick wash-up and get into bed and stay there.

CLIFFORD *(Considers, smiles)* I'll buy that.
    (He moves away and exits up the stairs. The phone rings. SIDNEY *picks it up, holds it a moment while he gets into the right frame of mind, then raises it)*

SIDNEY Hello? . . . Yes, a bad one. I gave her mouth-to-mouth resuscitation for ten or fifteen minutes but . . . *(The grief of a bereaved husband begins to overwhelm him)* . . . it's no use, there's—nothing. She's been under the weather the past few days. I wanted to call you but she wouldn't let me; she said it was only . . .

(The curtain has fallen)

ACT
TWO

When the curtain rises, CLIFFORD *is hard at work and*
SIDNEY *isn't. They sit facing each other across a handsome old
partners' desk,* SIDNEY *at its right side,* CLIFFORD *at its left.
(The desk from Act One is gone.) The draperies are open to
bright morning sunlight.* CLIFFORD, *typing away like sixty
on an old black Smith-Corona, is in chinos, a shirt, and boots.*
SIDNEY, *lolling in his chair and feigning unconcern, is in his
cardigan and another turtleneck. There's a sheet of paper in
"Zenobia," but it's probably blank.*

God, how CLIFFORD *types! On and on, speech after speech.
Occasionally he backtracks to X out a few words; occasionally
he pauses for an instant of intense thought. But then it's on
and on, fast and expert and clattering.* SIDNEY *finds it harder
and harder to hide his irritation. He squirms, frets, grits his
teeth. Eventually he pecks out a word, mouthing the letters—
s-h-i-t—and sits back and glares at it.*

CLIFFORD *whips out the finished page, scans it, puts it down
on a Manila folder beside him and begins revising with a pen.*

SIDNEY   That must have been quite a welfare office.

CLIFFORD   It was. Everyone had a poignant story.
They're creating the play of their own accord.

SIDNEY   No notes? No outline?

CLIFFORD   This isn't a thriller, Sidney. It's not depend-
ent on intricate plotting and contrived theatrics.
These are real people. All I'm doing is bringing

65

them on and letting them spill out their dreams and frustrations, their anger at the bureaucracy.

SIDNEY   Joe Papp will have a messenger at the door any minute.

CLIFFORD   I *was* thinking of him as a possible producer. Do you know him?

SIDNEY   Slightly. Let me see a few pages.

CLIFFORD   Sure, if you'd like to. But I'd really rather wait till the draft is done—give you the whole thing in one glorious bundle. Would you mind?

SIDNEY   Of course not. What's another hour or so?

CLIFFORD *(Putting a fresh sheet of paper into his typewriter)* It's going to take three or four weeks, I think.

SIDNEY   At the rate you're going you'll have a trilogy by then.

CLIFFORD   *(Looks sympathetically at him)* Nothing doing?

SIDNEY   I'm thinking . . .

CLIFFORD   Why don't you invite her over? Ten Dorp. Talking with her might spark something.

SIDNEY   Do you think we should risk having her on the premises?

CLIFFORD   Maybe not when the moon is full, but any other time, why not? Look at the egg she laid on the Griffin show.

SIDNEY   Well, she got rattled by Peter Hurkos when he described all her husbands in such detail.

CLIFFORD   Oh, Belle Forrester called before you came down. *(Resumes typing)* Wanted to know if she could bring over a casserole or come sew a button. I told her we were managing just fine.
> *(The doorbell chimes.* CLIFFORD *starts to rise but* SIDNEY *puts up a hand)*

SIDNEY   Don't. We don't want to break the flow, do we? *(He heads for the foyer.* CLIFFORD *resumes typing.* SIDNEY *opens the front door.* PORTER MILGRIM *is there, a man of substance in his mid-fifties; in hat, topcoat, and business suit, carrying a briefcase)* Porter! It's good to see you! Come on in.
> *(They shake hands)*

PORTER   How are you, Sidney?

SIDNEY   Doing fairly well, thanks.

PORTER *(Entering the foyer)*   There are a couple of things I want to talk to you about. Am I disturbing you?

SIDNEY *(Closing the door)*   Not at all. Glad of the chance to take a break. *(*PORTER *has put his briefcase down and is taking his hat and coat off)* How come you're not in the city?

PORTER   I have to be in New Haven this afternoon. The secretary?

SIDNEY *(Taking the hat and coat)*   Yes.

67

PORTER My, what a fast typist.
    (He picks up his briefcase while SIDNEY *hangs the hat and coat on a wall rack)*

SIDNEY He is, isn't he? Come meet him. Clifford?
    *(*CLIFFORD *stops typing; turns and rises as* PORTER *and* SIDNEY *come into the study)* This is Clifford Anderson. And this is my friend Porter Milgrim.

PORTER *(Shaking hands with* CLIFFORD*)* How do you do.

CLIFFORD How do you do, sir.

SIDNEY I would say "my attorney," but then he would bill me.

PORTER I'm going to, anyway; this is a business call. Partly, at least.

SIDNEY Clifford was at the seminar I conducted last July. He asked me then about a secretarial position, and . . . when Myra passed on . . . I realized I would need someone to lend a hand, so I called him. The next day, here he was.

CLIFFORD Have typewriter, will travel.

PORTER That was very good of you.

CLIFFORD It's a privilege to be of help to someone like Mr. Bruhl.

PORTER *(Noticing the desk)* Oh, look at that. Isn't this a beauty!

SIDNEY Partners' desk.

PORTER   Mmm! Where did you find it?

SIDNEY   In Wilton. Just happened on it last week. Makes more sense than cluttering the room with two single ones.

PORTER   Cost a pretty penny, I'll bet.

SIDNEY   Well, it's deductible.

PORTER   Yes, they can't very well quibble about a writer's desk, can they? Wait till Elizabeth sees this . . .

SIDNEY   How is she?

PORTER   Fine.

SIDNEY   And the girls?

PORTER   Couldn't be better. Cathy loves Vassar.

SIDNEY   And Vassar versa, I'm sure. Sit down.

CLIFFORD   Shall I go get the groceries now? Then you and Mr. Milgrim can talk in private.
        (SIDNEY *looks to* PORTER, *who nods infinitesimally*)

SIDNEY   Would you mind?

CLIFFORD   I have to do it sometime before dinner; might as well.

SIDNEY   All right. *(Heading for the foyer)* Be with you in a second, Porter.

PORTER   Take your time. I haven't started the clock yet! (SIDNEY *is out and on his way upstairs.* CLIFFORD

69

smiles as he rolls the paper from his typewriter. PORTER
sits and puts his briefcase down) I love this room.

CLIFFORD   Isn't it nice? It's a pleasure working here.
*(Puts the paper and the page he finished earlier into
the folder, behind other sheets in it)*

PORTER   He's looking well.

CLIFFORD   Yes, he's picked up quite a bit in the past
few days. *(Putting the folder into the desk)* It was pretty
bad the first week. He cried every night; I could
hear him plainly. And he was drinking heavily.

PORTER   Ah.

CLIFFORD   *(Standing against the desk)*   But he'll pull
through. His work is a great solace to him.

PORTER   I'm sure it must be. I've always envied my
writer clients on that account. *I* tried a play
once.

CLIFFORD   Oh?

PORTER   About the Supreme Court Justice I most
admire. But even the title was a problem. *Frankfurter . . .*
(He shakes his head ruefully. CLIFFORD *moves toward
the doorway as* SIDNEY *comes in, wallet in hand)*

SIDNEY   Twenty enough?

CLIFFORD   Too much; we only need salad things and
milk. I'm going to Gibson's.
(He goes into the foyer)

SIDNEY *(Pocketing his wallet)* Pick up some yogurt too. Anything but prune.

CLIFFORD *(Taking a jacket from the rack)* Okay. *(Putting the jacket on; to* PORTER*)* You aren't in the driveway, are you?

PORTER No, I pulled over on the side.

CLIFFORD See you later or nice meeting you, which-ever it turns out to be.
(He takes car keys from his pocket)

PORTER I'm sure we'll be seeing each other again. *(*CLIFFORD *nods to* SIDNEY *and goes out, closing the door behind him)* Pleasant young fellow. Good-looking too.

SIDNEY Yes . . . *(Turns to* PORTER*)* Do you think he's gay? Homosexual?

PORTER I know what "gay" means, Sidney. Elizabeth told me long ago. No, he didn't strike me that way.

SIDNEY I have a sneaking suspicion he might be. But as long as he does his job well, I suppose it's none of my business, is it?

PORTER Well, in essence he's a domestic employee, and I think that in such circumstances his sexual preference could be a legitimate matter of concern.

SIDNEY I wasn't asking for a legal opinion; I was just saying that it's really not my business.

PORTER Oh. In that case, no, it isn't.

SIDNEY *(Turning his desk chair to face* PORTER *and sitting)* Besides, people would talk if I took in a female secretary, wouldn't they?

PORTER   If she were under eighty.

SIDNEY   That's what I thought. So I called Clifford.

PORTER   I'm glad to see you looking so well. That's the main reason I've come. I was delegated, by Elizabeth and the Wessons and the Harveys. That young man has been discouraging all callers, and we were afraid you might be in worse shape than he was letting on. But obviously that's not the case.

SIDNEY   No. I'm not up to socializing yet but . . . I'm coming through. *(Touching the typewriter)* The work is a great solace to me.

PORTER   What are you onto now?

SIDNEY   A play about ESP. Helga ten Dorp is in the McBain cottage, you know.

PORTER   Yes, I do. Tell me, is it true what everyone's saying, that . . . Do you mind talking about this?

SIDNEY   No, no, not at all. Go ahead.

PORTER   Is it true she actually pointed to the spot on the floor where Myra was going to fall?

SIDNEY   No, no, no, no, no, no, no. Nothing like that, nothing at *all* like that. All she did was come in here and say, "There is pain, there is great pain. In this lady's chest." And Myra said, "There's *slight* pain," and she said, "Still, with your history you should see your doctor." Which is what I'd been telling Myra for days.

PORTER *(Picking up his briefcase)* It's uncanny being able to sense things that way. I would think you'd be able to write a very fine thriller on the subject.

SIDNEY It's coming along. *(PORTER glances at his watch and starts opening the briefcase.* SIDNEY *smiles)* Business time.

PORTER Yes. The first item on the agenda is your will. Now that Myra's gone you ought to look it over. As it stands, if anything should happen to you, your cousins in Vancouver would inherit. Do you want to leave it that way?

(He takes a couple of sheets of typewritten paper from his briefcase)

SIDNEY I don't know. I'll have to think about it.

PORTER Do. Don't put it off. And this is the second item. *(Hands him the papers)* It's only approximate, because I don't have up-to-date appraisals on the real estate yet, but that's roughly what you can anticipate, give or take a few thousand dollars.

SIDNEY *(Looks over the pages, and is somewhat surprised)* I didn't know there was this much . . .

PORTER Then Myra must have been keeping a few secrets. *She* knew; her records were in apple-pie order.

SIDNEY   How much of this is the government going to grab?

PORTER   Not too much, really. The first two hundred and fifty thousand of that is exempt from federal taxes, and the state tax, which starts at fifty thousand, is only a few percent.

SIDNEY   Hmm!

PORTER *(Closing his briefcase)*   There's one more point, Sidney. I was talking to Maury Escher at the Planning Board meeting last night, and he told me you spoke to him about selling off a few acres.

SIDNEY *(Looking at the papers)*   I'm not sure that I will now.

PORTER   You can't; not yet, anyway. You'll have to wait till the will goes through probate.

SIDNEY   I know that. I just asked him what he thought I could get.

PORTER   Oh. Then *he* was jumping the gun, not you. I wanted to make sure you were clear on the point. *(SIDNEY folds the papers thoughtfully and puts them into the desk. PORTER looks at his watch)* End of business. You've gotten off cheap.

SIDNEY *(Turns, smiles)*   Yes. I'm lucky.
     (PORTER rises; SIDNEY does too)

PORTER   What's the procedure? You dictate and he types?

SIDNEY   No, no, I do my own typing. I'll have him retype the finished product, of course. And he does the letters.

PORTER *(Has paused by the desk)*   Is that what he was doing before? Letters?

SIDNEY   No, a play of his own.

PORTER   Oh, the seminar—of course.

SIDNEY   Started it yesterday and will probably finish it tomorrow.
     (He expects PORTER *to move on, but* PORTER *stays studying the desk)*

PORTER   I hope he's not stealing your ESP idea . . . Have you discussed it with him?

SIDNEY *(Looks at him for a moment)*   What makes you say that?

PORTER   He locked what he was working on into the drawer. Unobtrusively, but I noticed.
     *(*SIDNEY *looks at him for another moment, and frowning, goes to* CLIFFORD's *side of the desk. He tries the center drawer; it's locked)*

SIDNEY   Hmm.

PORTER   Then again, he might be afraid *you'll* steal *his* idea.

SIDNEY   Hardly. Life at a welfare office: the dreams and frustrations of half a dozen people you'd just as soon not spend an evening with.

PORTER   He's worked in a welfare office?

SIDNEY   Yes, that's what he was doing.
          (He tries the drawer again)

PORTER   It might only be force of habit, then. People
in large offices often lock their desks.

SIDNEY   Unobtrusively? Just the reverse, I'd think.
"Hey, everybody, look, I'm locking my desk!"

PORTER   It may simply be his way of doing things.
(SIDNEY drums uneasily on the desktop) I'm sorry if I've
worried you. The suspicious legal mind. Probably
he's exactly what he seems: an honest and helpful
young man, completely trustworthy.

SIDNEY   Yes. Probably.

PORTER   Well, I'd better get moving if I'm going to be
in New Haven by noon. *(He heads for the foyer; SID-
NEY pulls himself away from the desk and goes after him)*
Trustees' luncheon at Old Eli. *(PORTER removes his
coat from the rack; SIDNEY takes it and holds it for him)*
Thanks. Has the check from the insurance company
come yet?

SIDNEY   No, it hasn't.

PORTER   I'll write them a letter first thing in the
morning.

SIDNEY *(Giving him his hat)*   Thanks. I'd appreciate it.

PORTER   Will you come have dinner with us?

SIDNEY   In another week or two I think I'll be ready
to face the world again.
(He opens the door)

PORTER   Good enough. Take care.

SIDNEY   You too. *(PORTER goes out)* Give my love to
Elizabeth.

PORTER *(Offstage)*   I will.

SIDNEY   And the girls! *(He stands watching for a moment,
and then he closes the door and turns. He comes slowly into
the study and stands looking at CLIFFORD's side of the desk;
picks up something on it, examines it, puts it down; drums
on the desktop; frowns. He gets his keys out, chooses a likely
one, and tries it; it won't go in. He chooses another, and
tries again, more carefully; same result. He pockets the
keys, frowning—and then smiles. Going up around the
desk, he takes the key from the drawer on his side and
continues down and around to CLIFFORD's side. He puts the
key in; it won't turn)* Shit. *(He tries again, without luck.
Taking the key out, he goes back to his side and replaces it;
thinks a second and moves toward the wall of weapons. He
takes down a flat-bladed stiletto; back to the desk. Sitting
in CLIFFORD's chair, he sets to work with the stiletto;
inserts it above the drawer and pokes and levers)* Come
on, you bastard . . . Goddamned Old World crafts-
men. *(He keeps trying, but it's no use. Defeated, he gets
up and puts the stiletto back in its place; looks at the desk
and is inspired. Going quickly to his side of it, he moves
the chair away, takes out the center drawer, and puts it*

down across the chair arms. Getting down on his knees, he peers into the drawer-opening, then thrusts his arm into it and reaches as far as he can. He switches arms and tries harder, sweating a bit but apparently near success) Ah, ah, ah, ah . . . Ooh, ooh, ooh, ooh! *(It would seem his fingers are caught)* Oh my God! Oh Jesus Christmas! *(Now he's really sweating, glancing at the door and wincing and straining as he tries to extricate his arm from the desk's maw. After considerable effort he manages to do so. Sucking his injured fingers, he stands up, kicks the desk, examines his fingers, wipes them under his arm. He picks up the drawer and fits it back into the desk, slamming it home with a vengeance. He hears something; hurries to the front door and jumps up to look through the fanlight, then hurries back into the study; anguishes over the desk in last-ditch frustration)* Feces! *(But then he runs to the French doors, unbolts and opens them a bit; runs back to his side of the desk, opens a drawer and takes out a Manila folder; opens another drawer and takes out a dozen or so sheets of typing paper. He shoves the paper into the folder, puts it down, closes the drawers, partly covers the folder with a loose piece of paper as* CLIFFORD *unlocks the front door and comes in with a bag of groceries)* That was quick!

CLIFFORD   I only went to Gibson's.
(He closes the door. SIDNEY *goes briskly and cheerfully to him)*

SIDNEY   Here, give me; I'll put them away.

CLIFFORD   It's all right, I don't mind.

SIDNEY *(Taking the bag)* No, no, come on. You shopped; I'll put away. Get back to the welfare office.

CLIFFORD God forbid. *(SIDNEY goes off to the right. CLIFFORD takes some bills and coins from his jacket pocket, puts them down)* The change is in the bowl. *(Takes his jacket off, hangs it on the rack; looks off to the right)* The avocado is supposed to be organic.

> *(SIDNEY says something unintelligible but affirmative-sounding. CLIFFORD comes into the study, tucking his shirt down into his chinos and taking a key from his pocket. He sits at the desk, puts the key into the lock, unlocks and opens the drawer; takes out his folder, closes the drawer. He leafs through the folder, takes out the bottom partly done page, and scanning it, puts the folder down at his left. He scans the page for another moment, then rolls it into the typewriter and positions it with care so that the new typing will be aligned with the old. He studies the page, thinks a bit, and begins typing. He types several words)*

SIDNEY *(Offstage)* Cliff! *(CLIFFORD stops typing)* Would you give me a hand here?

> *(CLIFFORD gets up and heads for the foyer. As he enters it and starts off to the right SIDNEY comes racing through the French doors. He switches the two folders)*

CLIFFORD *(Offstage)* Where are you?

> *(SIDNEY pulls a bottle of beer from his hip pocket)*

SIDNEY Where are *you?*
>   *(He ambles on toward the foyer.* CLIFFORD *comes in through the French doors)*

CLIFFORD Hey, wait!

SIDNEY *(Turning)* Oh, there you are. I didn't think you heard, so I came around. *(They head toward each other,* SIDNEY *holding out the beer)* Need those Olympic fingers.

CLIFFORD Beer now?
>   *(He takes the bottle)*

SIDNEY Got a sudden mad craving, as in the commercials. Shook it a bit—sorry.

CLIFFORD *(Opens the beer, hands him the bottle and cap)* You can use an opener on these.

SIDNEY Really?

CLIFFORD *(Getting a handkerchief from his pocket)* Sure. Doesn't it say so?

SIDNEY *(Trying to focus on the cap)* Who do they expect to read this, roaches? *(Still trying to read the cap, he goes to the foyer and off to the right.* CLIFFORD, *wiping his hands, sits down again, pockets the handkerchief, studies the page, and resumes typing. After a few moments* SIDNEY *comes strolling in through the foyer, carefully pouring beer into a pilsner glass.* CLIFFORD *types away at full speed.* SIDNEY, *getting the head just right, sits in his chair, sets the bottle on the desk, and admires the beer's color and effervescence. He tries a sip, gives it tentative approval; leans back and takes a longer sip. Yes, definitely good stuff. Casually he reaches out and takes the folder from the desk, puts it on his lap. Another sip. He opens the folder. His eyes bulge. He almost chokes but manages somehow to get the beer down. He turns to the next page. Worse news here! He glances incredulously at* CLIFFORD, *who's typing, typing, typing.* SIDNEY *turns to the next page: still worse and more of it. He reads, aghast and aghaster. He puts the glass on the desk, with another shocked glance at* CLIFFORD, *and looks through the remaining dozen pages, reading bits here and there and mouthing "Oh my God!" and such. He closes the folder, closes his eyes, sits motionless for a moment; opens his eyes, puts the folder on the desk, and sits staring at* CLIFFORD *as at Judas Iscariot or worse.* CLIFFORD *whips the finished page from the typewriter, scans it, puts it down on the folder beside him and begins penning revisions.* SIDNEY *watches him, picks up the beer glass, sips)* So you've lost your interest in thrillers, eh?

CLIFFORD Mmm.

SIDNEY *(Another sip)* No taste for the intricate plotting and the glib superficial characters . . .

CLIFFORD Mm-hmm.

SIDNEY Want to do something real and meaningful, socially relevant.

CLIFFORD *(Turning, smiling understandingly)* Hey, cut it out, will you? Your idea'll start coming.

SIDNEY Possibly . . .

CLIFFORD   Just relax, and don't try to bug *me*. It'll
come.

> (*He returns to his revising.* SIDNEY *puts the glass
> down and picks up the folder; puts it on his lap, opens
> it, reads*)

SIDNEY   "*Deathtrap:* A Thriller in Two Acts." (CLIF-
FORD *looks up, wide-eyed. He turns;* SIDNEY *smiles at him
and turns to the next page*) "Characters: Julian Crane,
Doris Crane, Willard Peterson, Inga van Bronk."
(CLIFFORD *whips his folder open; and closes it*) "The
action takes place in Julian Crane's study, in the
Crane home in Westport, Connecticut."

> (*He turns the page*)

CLIFFORD   *You have one hell of a nerve stealing—*

SIDNEY (*Cutting him off fortissimo*)   "SETTING! Julian
Crane's study is a handsomely converted stable
grafted onto an authentically Colonial house! Sliding doors upstage center (*Pointing at them*) open on
a foyer in which are the house's front door, entrances to the living room and kitchen, and the stairway to the second floor! French doors upstage right
(*Pointing*) open out to a shrubbery-flanked patio!
Downstage left (*And pointing again*) is a fieldstone
fireplace, *practical to the extent that PAPER CAN BE
BURNED IN IT! (He rises.* CLIFFORD *is resignedly riding
out the storm.* SIDNEY *gives a guided tour of the room,
folder in hand*) "The room's furnishings are tastefully chosen antiques: a few chairs and occasional
pieces, a buffet downstage right, with liquor decan-

ters, and—the focus of the room—Julian's desk."
You remember Julian's desk, don't you? *The one he
worked at before he took Crazy Willard Peterson into
his home?* "Patterned draperies hang at the French
doors. The room is decorated with framed theatrical posters"—unlike these, which are *window
cards*, not *posters!*—"and a collection of guns,
handcuffs, maces, broadswords, and battle-axes"—
several of which I'm going to make use of any
minute now.

(*He closes the folder, stands glaring at* CLIFFORD)

CLIFFORD   That's it? You're not going to act out the
eleven pages? Would you like me to explain?

SIDNEY   What's to explain? You're a lunatic with a
death wish; Freud covered it thoroughly.

CLIFFORD   I have exactly the same wish you have: a
success wish.

SIDNEY   *This* is going to bring you success?

CLIFFORD   It hit me that night. Remember, I put in
that extra speech when you were looking for the
key? It can be a terrific thriller.

SIDNEY   In which someone like me and someone like
you give someone like Myra a fatal heart attack?

CLIFFORD   Yes. At the end of Act One.

SIDNEY   What, pray tell, is your *definition* of success?
Being gang-banged in the shower room at the state
penitentiary?

83

CLIFFORD   I knew you would have reservations about it; that's why my first instinct was to say it wasn't even a thriller. I haven't enjoyed putting you on, Sidney. I'm glad it's out in the open.

SIDNEY   You knew I would have reservations . . .

CLIFFORD   Well, you do, don't you?

SIDNEY   The house madman is writing a play that'll send both of us to prison—

CLIFFORD   It won't!

SIDNEY   —I'm standing here terrified, petrified, horrified, stupefied, *crapping my pants*—and he calls that "having reservations." I'm not going to use one of *those* on you; I'm going to beat you to death with *Roget's Thesaurus*!

CLIFFORD   There is no possible way for anyone to prove what did or did not cause Myra's heart attack. Look, if I could change things I would, but I can't; it *has* to be a playwright. Who else can pretend to receive a finished work that could make tons of money?

SIDNEY   A novelist! A composer! Why am I discussing this?

CLIFFORD   A sure-fire smash-hit symphony? No. And would a novelist or a composer know where to get a garrotte that squirts blood, and how to stage a convincing murder? And it has to be a playwright *who writes thrillers,* because Arthur Miller probably has old sample cases hanging on his wall . . . I *suppose* I could make it Wilton instead of Westport . . .

SIDNEY   Why make it *anywhere? Why make it?*

CLIFFORD   It's *there*, Sidney!

SIDNEY   That's mountains, not plays! Plays aren't there till some asshole writes them!

CLIFFORD   Stop and think for a minute, will you? Think. About that night. Try to see it all from an audience's viewpoint. *Everything we did to convince Myra that she was seeing a real murder would have exactly the same effect on them.* Weren't *we* giving a play? Didn't we write it, rehearse it? Wasn't *she* our audience? *(He rises.* SIDNEY *is listening as one fascinated by a lunatic's raving)* Scene One: Julian tells Doris about this terrific play that's come in the mail. He jokes about killing for it, then calls Willard and invites him over, getting him to bring the original copy. Audience thinks exactly what Doris thinks: Julian might kill Willard. Scene Two: *everything that happened from the moment we came through that door.* All the little ups and downs we put in to make it ring true: the I'm-expecting-a-phone-call bit, everything. Tightened up a little, naturally. And then the strangling, which scares the audience as much as it does Doris.

SIDNEY   No wonder you didn't need an outline.

CLIFFORD   *(Tapping his temple)*   It's all up here, every bit of it. Scene Three: "Inga van Bronk." A few laughs, right? Can't hurt. Then Julian and Doris get ready to go upstairs—it looks as if the act is drawing to a kind of so-so close—and pow, in comes Willard, out of the grave and seeking vengeance. Shock? Surprise? Doris has her heart attack, Julian gets up from the fake beating—and the audience realizes that Julian and Willard are in cahoots, that there isn't any sure-fire thriller, that Willard is moving in. The curtain is Julian burning the manuscripts. Or calling the doctor—I'm not sure which. Now be honest about it: isn't that a sure-fire first act?

SIDNEY   Yes. And what an intermission. Twenty years to life.

CLIFFORD   No one can prove it really happened. They *can't.* How can they?

SIDNEY   And what do you say to the man from the *Times,* when he says, "Don't you work for Sidney Bruhl, and didn't his wife have a heart attack just around the time you came there?"

CLIFFORD   (*Turning out his hands for the obvious answer*) "No comment."

SIDNEY   Oh my God . . .
     (*Moves about in futility*)

CLIFFORD   I know it's going to be a little sticky, but—well, everybody's opening up about everything these days, aren't they? In print, on TV; why not on stage, as long as it can't be proved? I've given it some serious thought, Sidney, and I honestly believe it'll *help* the play, give it an added dimension of . . . intriguing gossip.

SIDNEY   I'm sure you're right. I can see the little box in *New York* magazine now: "Tongues are wagging about interesting similarities between events in the new play *Deathtrap* and the private lives of its author Clifford Anderson and his employer Sidney Bruhl, who committed suicide on opening night. When queried, Mr. Anderson said, 'No comment.' " *I* have a comment, Cliff. No. Absolutely, definitely *no*. I have a name and a reputation—tattered, perhaps, but still valid for dinner invitations, house seats, and the conducting of summer seminars. I want to live out my years as "author of *The Murder Game*," not "fag who knocked off his wife." *(Turns to the right)* Why, look—a fieldstone fireplace! *(Heading for it, folder at the ready)* Let's see if it's practical to the extent that paper—

CLIFFORD *(Interrupting him)*   *DON'T YOU DARE!* *(*SID-NEY *stops)* You burn that—and I go out of here and write it again somewhere else. I'll . . . get a house-sitting job. *(Goes to* SIDNEY *and puts out his hand)* Give it to me. Give it, Sidney. *(*SIDNEY *turns and hands the folder to* CLIFFORD*)* I helped you kill for the chance to become what I want to be. You're not going to take it away from me. *(He goes to the desk.* SIDNEY *watches him)* I had *hoped* that when I showed you the finished draft, you would be impressed enough to . . . get over your *Angel Street* uptightness and pitch in, but I guess we can forget about *that*.

87

SIDNEY *(Smiles faintly)* A collaboration?

CLIFFORD It's mostly your idea, isn't it? I'm not pretending it's all my baby. And I know that Scene One is coming out a little . . . heavy and stilted. I hoped we could be a team, Bruhl and Anderson.

SIDNEY Rodgers and Heartless.

CLIFFORD Now you see, I could never come up with something like that.

SIDNEY I'm sorry, but I really don't feel like collaborating on my public humiliation.

CLIFFORD Next season's hit. Don't say I didn't ask. *(SIDNEY moves away, perturbed. CLIFFORD, standing by the desk playing with the folder, glances at him, and at the folder again)* I think maybe I'd better move out anyway . . .

SIDNEY Why?

CLIFFORD When Helga ten Dorp said a woman was going to use the dagger because of a play—maybe she really wasn't that far off target.
(SIDNEY stands silently for a moment. CLIFFORD toys with the folder)

SIDNEY Don't be silly. I . . . I love you; I wouldn't think of . . . trying to harm you. Besides, you'd break my neck.

CLIFFORD Goddamn right I would.

SIDNEY So don't talk about leaving.

CLIFFORD   I don't know . . . I'm not going to feel comfortable with you being unhappy about this.

SIDNEY   I'll whistle a lot. *(He comes to the desk.* CLIFFORD *riffles through the pages in the folder.* SIDNEY *throws a quick worried glance at him, then looks thoughtfully into space)* Maybe I *am* being—old-fashioned and uptight.

CLIFFORD   You are. These days, jeez, who cares about anything?

SIDNEY   I certainly could *use* half the royalties of a good solid hit . . .

CLIFFORD   I think there's a movie in it too.

SIDNEY   Porter just gave me the figures on Myra's estate. It's even smaller than I thought. Twenty-two thousand dollars, half of which goes in taxes. There's the house and land, of course, but I can't sell any acreage until the will goes through probate, and he says that's going to take two or three years.

CLIFFORD   Whew.

SIDNEY   The insurance money isn't all that much.

CLIFFORD   *(Moving to his chair)*   The offer is still open. *(He sits)*

SIDNEY   You know, it crossed my mind that afternoon that the play-in-the-mail thing would make a good first scene . . . Really.

CLIFFORD It's *your idea*, Sidney. All I did was help with some of the details. *(SIDNEY, wrestling visibly with a difficult decision, sits at his side of the desk. CLIFFORD hands across the folder of blank papers. SIDNEY takes it, smiles)* Pretty neat, the way you managed it.

SIDNEY I tried breaking in; the damn thing's a fortress. Porter noticed you locking up. I was afraid you were doing something on ESP.

CLIFFORD And I thought I was being so inconspicuous.

SIDNEY He's sharp. Dull, but sharp. *(CLIFFORD smiles, and looks at his finished page. SIDNEY weighs his decision)* I'll do it. *Let* people talk; I'll blush all the way to the bank.

CLIFFORD You mean it?

SIDNEY Bruhl and Anderson.

CLIFFORD Great! *(He extends his hand; SIDNEY shakes it across the desktop, and they add a warm extra handclasp. CLIFFORD sits back happily)* We'll make it Wilton, not Westport.

SIDNEY Leave it Westport—the hell with it.

CLIFFORD Jesus, just think: me, Clifford Anderson, collaborating with Sidney Bruhl!

SIDNEY That's from Act One.

CLIFFORD *(Smiles, and then grows sober)* Act Two is going to be a problem . . .

SIDNEY How so?

CLIFFORD Well, we've got the murder in Act One. Two murders, in effect. Act Two is liable to be a letdown.

SIDNEY Not—necessarily . . .

CLIFFORD *(Rolling a sheet of paper into his typewriter)* We'll bring in a detective, of course—the fifth character. I was thinking of a Connecticut version of the one in *Dial "M."*

SIDNEY Inspector Hubbard.

CLIFFORD Yeh. And Inga van Bronk ought to come in again. A good comic character like that, it would be foolish not to make the most of her.

SIDNEY You go on drafting Act One. Let *me* do a little thinking about Act Two . . .
> *(CLIFFORD smiles at him, glances at his finished page, and begins typing. SIDNEY looks sorrowfully at him for a moment, then picks up his beer, leans back in his chair, and thinks, thinks, thinks as the lights fade to darkness)*

SCENE TWO

When the lights come up, CLIFFORD, *in a different shirt, is standing at his side of the desk squaring up a sizable thickness of paper and looking pleased with himself.* SIDNEY's *typewriter is covered;* CLIFFORD's *isn't. The room is quite dark; the desk lamp and a light outside the front-door fanlight are the only illumination. Wind can be heard. Through the darkness outside the closed French doors a flashlight approaches; the person holding it raps at the doors.* CLIFFORD *starts. He puts the papers down, and as the person raps again, goes warily toward the doors.*

HELGA *(Shining the flashlight onto her face)* Mr. Bruhl? Is I, Helga ten Dorp!
> (CLIFFORD *turns a lamp on and goes and unbolts the French doors and opens them)*

CLIFFORD Come in. Mr. Bruhl isn't here now.

HELGA *(Coming in, in a raincoat and kerchief)* I come through wood; is less to walk.

CLIFFORD *(Closing the doors)* He should be back any minute.

HELGA You are?

CLIFFORD His secretary, Clifford Anderson.

HELGA *(Offers her hand)* I am Helga ten Dorp. I am psychic.

92

CLIFFORD *(Shaking her hand)* I know, Mr. Bruhl's told me about you. I understand you predicted his wife's death.

HELGA *(Coming into the room, pocketing her flashlight)* Ja, ja, was much pain. Right here. *(Pats her chest)* Very sad. Such a nice lady. *Ei*, this room . . . He is well, Mr. Bruhl?

CLIFFORD Yes, fine. He went out to dinner, the first time since . . . He said he'd be back by ten and it's about a quarter past now.

HELGA Will be big storm! Much wind and rain, lightning and thunder. Trees will fall.

CLIFFORD Are you sure?

HELGA *Ja*, was on radio. *(Takes her kerchief off)* I come to borrow candles. Are none in house. You have?

CLIFFORD I don't know. I haven't noticed any but there must be some. I'll go look. Why don't you sit down?

HELGA Thank you. (CLIFFORD *starts for the foyer.* HELGA *starts to sit but rises, pointing)* You wear boots!
     (CLIFFORD *stops, and after a moment turns)*

CLIFFORD Everyone does these days. They're very comfortable.

HELGA You are for long time secretary to Mr. Bruhl?

CLIFFORD No. I just came here . . . about three weeks ago. After Mrs. Bruhl died. (HELGA *turns from him, worried and perplexed)* I'll go look for—

93

(He is interrupted by the unlocking and opening of the front door. SIDNEY *comes in, switching the foyer light on and the outside light off. He's in a trenchcoat over a shirt, tie, and jacket)*

SIDNEY *(Closing the door)* Hi. What a bore *that*—

CLIFFORD *(Interrupting him)* Mr. Bruhl! Hello. Mrs. ten Dorp is here.
(He and SIDNEY *exchange a look)*

SIDNEY Oh. *(Comes to the doorway, smiling)* Hello.

HELGA *(Going toward him)* Good evening, Mr. Bruhl.

SIDNEY *(Meeting her, shaking her hand)* How are you?

HELGA Well.

SIDNEY Did you get my note?

HELGA *Ja,* thank you.

SIDNEY *(Taking his coat off)* Yours was most kind. And the flowers . . .

CLIFFORD Do we have any candles? There's a storm coming up and Mrs. ten Dorp wants to borrow some.

SIDNEY Yes, we've got a box of them somewhere. I think Myra kept them over the refrigerator. If not there, then on the shelf on the landing. *(*CLIFFORD *goes off to the right.* SIDNEY *moves back into the foyer)* A gray cardboard box. *(Hangs his coat on the rack)* I saw you on the Griffin show. It wasn't a very good night, was it? *(But* HELGA *is urgently gesturing for him to come in and close the door. He does so)* What is it?

HELGA *(Whispering)* Is man I warn you of! Man in boots who attacks you!

SIDNEY *(Is caught off guard, then thinks)* Oh my God. In the . . . turmoil of Myra's death, I completely forgot about that warning!
(The wind blows)

HELGA Is *he!* Candles are not why I come! Have many candles! But tonight I feel here danger again, and in this room is feeling very strong! You should not have him here!

SIDNEY Do you know, I made up my mind just tonight to dismiss him? I was discussing the matter with my lawyer. I became uneasy about him last week, so I asked my lawyer to do a—

HELGA *(Interrupting him)* Ei! *(Peers at* CLIFFORD's *typewriter)* Smith-Corona! *(Looks at* SIDNEY*)* Is his?

SIDNEY *Ja.* Yes!

HELGA But naturally! *Corona,* not *Colonna! Ach! This* is why I see on black man's face "qwertyuiop"! You must send away this man tonight!

SIDNEY I was going to—to give him his notice, at any rate. And I certainly won't put it off, now that you've come and warned me about him. You're positive you saw him attacking me?

HELGA Was image like TV, so sharp!
  (CLIFFORD, *coming out of the kitchen, hesitates*)

SIDNEY Come in, Clifford!
  (CLIFFORD *comes in with an open box of candles. He brings them to* HELGA, *who smiles tautly and avoids his eyes*)

HELGA Thank you. I take two.

SIDNEY You're welcome to take more.

HELGA No, two are enough.

CLIFFORD *(Withdrawing a few steps)* It's really blowing up out there.

HELGA *(Pocketing the candles)* *Ja*, sometime they are right with their predictions. *(Ready to tie her kerchief; to* SIDNEY, *sotto voce)* I should stay?

SIDNEY *(Sotto)* No need to. *(And aloud)* I hope you beat the rain.
  (*He moves toward the foyer*)

HELGA I go through wood; is less to walk. *(To* CLIFFORD*)* Good night.

CLIFFORD Good night.

SIDNEY *(Opening the French doors)* It's pitch-black. Will you be able to find your way?

HELGA *Ja*, I have torch.
  (*She gets out her flashlight*)

SIDNEY Good night. *(HELGA stops, turns, gasps)* What's wrong?

> *(CLIFFORD moves closer; he and SIDNEY exchange worried looks as HELGA stays speechless for another moment)*

HELGA My daughter is pregnant! Ohhhhh! So many years they try! So many doctors they go to! And now, at last, they make me grandmother! *Ei! Goddank! Goddank! (Another stunning realization lights her face)* I must call and tell them!

> *(She hurries out. SIDNEY, smiling, closes the doors and bolts them, draws the draperies)*

CLIFFORD She told you I'm the man in boots who attacks you?

SIDNEY Yes.

CLIFFORD She noticed them just before you came in. *(Smiles)* Did you tell her I used a styrofoam log, not one of the weapons?

SIDNEY Didn't think it quite advisable. I told her you're giving me karate lessons and we're attacking each other all over the place. *(Smiles)* "The closer you stay to the truth, the better off you are."

CLIFFORD *(Putting the box of candles down)* I finished Act One.

SIDNEY Did you? *(CLIFFORD gestures at the desk. SIDNEY goes toward it)* Your evening was better spent than mine.

(He picks up the stack of paper and riffles through it.
CLIFFORD *comes over)*

CLIFFORD   I ended it with Julian on the phone.

SIDNEY *(Reads a line and looks doubtfully at* CLIFFORD*)*
"How can I go on without her?"

CLIFFORD   He wants the doctor to think he's upset,
doesn't he?

SIDNEY   Mmm. *(Putting the papers down)*   Well, your
dialogue may be a bit Tin Pan Alley but your timing
couldn't be better. I've got Act Two ready to go.

CLIFFORD   Terrific!
(A flash of lightning shines through the draperies)

SIDNEY   That is, I think I do. There are two bits of
business I'm not sure will work. We'll try them, and
if they do I'll give you the whole thing scene by
scene. It's full of surprises.

CLIFFORD   I can't wait to hear!
(A roll of thunder)

SIDNEY   Go up and check the windows first, will you?
It sounds as if we're getting hurricanes Alice
through Zelda.

CLIFFORD *(Heading for the foyer)*   How many scenes are
there?

SIDNEY   Three, same as in Act One. *(*CLIFFORD *goes
out and starts up the stairs)* I like that sort of sym-
metry . . .

(SIDNEY *stands for a moment, then takes his jacket off and hangs it on the back of his desk chair; adjusts it nicely. A brighter lightning flash. He goes to the fireplace, takes a pistol from over the mantel, aims it and mock-fires; then, in the light of the lamp, he carefully resets the safety catch. A roll of thunder, and the sound of rain falling. The storm grows in intensity through the balance of the scene. With the pistol ready for firing,* SIDNEY *places it on the mantel in easy picking-up position. He looks around, judging movements and relative locations, and satisfied, rubs his hands, hitches up his belt, and waits tensely. Footsteps sound on the stairs, and* CLIFFORD *comes in*)

CLIFFORD   All windows closed.

SIDNEY   Fine.

CLIFFORD   What are the bits of business?

SIDNEY   They're in the final scene, back to back, as it were. Willard has spilled the beans and our Connecticut version of Inspector Hubbard has come to beard Julian in his den. Julian, quite berserk, shoots the inspector in the left arm, but there's only one bullet in the gun, so now he's trying to get to the upstage wall in order to grab a weapon and finish the job. Question number one is: Can a one-armed inspector in otherwise good condition stop a two-armed middle-aged playwright from going where he wants? The answer had better be no. Let's try it. Me Julian, you Hubbard. Right about here . . .

CLIFFORD Left arm out of commission.

SIDNEY Yes. Ready?

CLIFFORD Ready.

(SIDNEY *starts toward* CLIFFORD, *who tries to stop him, using only his right arm.* SIDNEY *gets free fairly easily*)

SIDNEY You've got to try harder than that.

CLIFFORD That would look convincing, I think.

SIDNEY Not even to a theater party. Come on, give it a good try. *(They scuffle again, with more gusto and accompanied by some lightning and thunder.* SIDNEY *again gets free with relative ease)* Maybe *you* should be Julian.

CLIFFORD I was afraid I would tear your shirt.

SIDNEY Cliff, dear, we're trying to become rich and famous; let's not let a five-year-old shirt stand in the way, okay?

CLIFFORD Can't we just let the director and the actors work it out?

SIDNEY That isn't the way professional playwrights operate, dum-dum. Professional playwrights don't offer a script until they're absolutely sure that everything in it is playable and do-able. Now let's show 'em why Bruhl and Anderson are going to go down in theatrical history! *(They scuffle again, an earnest and fairly long struggle punctuated by exclamations and comments. At the end of it,* SIDNEY, *his shirt torn, manages to thrust* CLIFFORD *away and get to the wall of weapons) Voilà!* It works!

CLIFFORD *(Pulling himself together)* And look at your shirt. And mine. Jesus! *(SIDNEY comes toward him)* I scratched your neck.

SIDNEY *(Wiping it with his hand)* I'll survive. The second bit now—much less strenuous and very brief.

CLIFFORD I'm glad of that.

SIDNEY I'm Hubbard now and you're Julian. Go on up to the wall. *(CLIFFORD does so)* Take the ax. *(CLIFFORD takes the ax from the wall and turns; holds it with both hands)* It doesn't look natural that way.

CLIFFORD It feels natural.

SIDNEY Try a different way.

CLIFFORD *(Shifts to another hold on the ax, and shakes his head)* It doesn't feel right this way.

SIDNEY All right, go back to the way you had it. *(CLIFFORD does so, waits)* Now put it down. On the floor. *(A bit puzzled,* CLIFFORD *obeys.* SIDNEY *turns and takes the pistol from the mantel, aims it at* CLIFFORD*)* Stand very still. We have good-byes to say. *(CLIFFORD's eyes widen) Deathtrap* is over. We're now into theater *vérité. (The storm gathers strength)* The gun from *Gunpoint.* No blanks as at the dear old Lyceum though—real bullets, courtesy of the Messrs. Remington. I loaded it last night, after you were asleep. I really don't want that play to be written.

Even though nothing can be proved, too much will be talked about, and I'm a little too old and, yes, uptight, to join the Washington secretaries, and the ex-lovers of ex-Presidents, and the happy hookers, and the happily hooked, in the National Bad-Taste Exposition. And I honestly can't think of any other way to make sure you won't set me up in a centrally located booth . . . I asked Porter to have you checked out in Hartford. A few blots were found on your record, precisely the ones you told me about, and Porter feels—we discussed it this evening—that they tend to justify the unease I've been feeling. So I came home and gave you your notice, you became abusive and violent, and Mrs. ten Dorp's three-week-old vision came to pass. Luckily I got to the gun, which I have the license and right to use in self-defense. It beats digging up the vegetable patch, doesn't it? I'm truly sorry, Cliff. If you hadn't succumbed to *thrilleritis malignis,* in what is *surely* one of the most acute cases on record, who knows, we might actually have *become* the team of Bruhl and Anderson. As it is, we'll have to be—only Bruhl. I'm out of dialogue. Your go.

CLIFFORD   What can I say? I'm not going to beg.

SIDNEY   I thought you might promise to become a steamfitter or something.

CLIFFORD   Would you believe me?

SIDNEY   No.

CLIFFORD   So? *(Shrugs)* I'm hoping you'll take pity on a pretty face.

SIDNEY   Oh God, I shall miss you very much. Good-bye, Cliff.

CLIFFORD   Good-bye, Sidney. (SIDNEY *hesitates an instant, then shoots; the blast is louder than the thunder.* CLIFFORD *stands for a moment and scratches himself*) I thought a click would be anticlimactic, so I bought some blanks this morning. While I was getting the bullets for this one. *(Takes a pistol from the wall and aims it at* SIDNEY) Sit down—dum-dum. (SIDNEY *stands staring at him*) Sit *down. Peripeteia?* Reversal? You talked about it the first day of the seminar. Important element of all drama. Put that down. (SIDNEY, *stunned, sits and puts the gun down.* CLIFFORD *draws a deep breath and moves from his fixed position, keeping the pistol trained on* SIDNEY) The problem was, I had this terrific first act, and I couldn't think of a second act. Very frustrating. Particularly since I'm sharing bed and board with the old master plotter himself, "author of *The Murder Game.*" And of *In for the Kill,* which I consider an even more elegant construction.

SIDNEY   Thanks, that makes two of us.

CLIFFORD *(Taking a pair of handcuffs from the wall)*   At present, yes. *(Approaching* SIDNEY) Be my guest. *(He offers the handcuffs)*

SIDNEY *(Mock-ingenuous)*   You mean put them on?

CLIFFORD   That's what I mean.
   (SIDNEY *resignedly takes the handcuffs and begins
   cuffing one wrist.* CLIFFORD *withdraws a bit*)

SIDNEY   What are you going to do?

CLIFFORD   Continue gloating. Through the arm of
   the chair. Don't play dumb! Through the arm!
   (Sighing, SIDNEY *passes the other cuff through the chair
   arm and locks it about his wrist.* CLIFFORD *sits on the
   corner of the desk)* So there I am with my problem.
   Sidney's not going to help me with it, not volun-
   tarily; this I know from square one. Sidney uses
   three kinds of deodorant and four kinds of
   mouthwash; not for him the whiff of scandal. But
   is there maybe a way I can *harness* that seventeen-
   jewel brain and set it to work for me all unwit-
   tingly? So I begin writing Act One, and every
   time I leave the desk, I inconspicuously lock the
   drawer. *So* inconspicuously, in fact, that for a day
   and a half smart Sidney doesn't notice. But dull
   old Porter comes in, thank God, and saves me the
   embarrassment of getting heavy-handed and leaving a loose page lying around.

SIDNEY   You're a shit, you know that?

CLIFFORD *(Raising the gun)*   Would you mind saying
   that into the microphone? So there we are, Bruhl
   and Anderson. I write, Sidney thinks. I don't sleep
   much—last night, for instance, I barely got a wink
   what with all the tiptoeing that was going on—but
   I'll make it up next week . . . Thank you for Act

Two. No Inspector Hubbard. Julian's lawyer is the fifth character. Scene One: Julian finds out that Willard is writing the real *Deathtrap* about Doris's murder. With changed names, of course. *(The storm is approaching its peak)* He pretends he'll collaborate, but asks old "Peter Pilgrim" or something to check up on Willard, knowing full well there are false and unfair charges to be found. Scene Two: Julian sets Willard up for what'll look like murder in self-defense by *getting him to enact bits of business for the play.* That's *beautiful,* Sidney! The whole thing we just did; it'll play like a dream and I *never* would have thought of it! I'm really in your debt. (SIDNEY *glares)* Julian shoots Willard, who's basically an innocent kid Julian led astray—

SIDNEY   Ooh, you bastard . . .

CLIFFORD   —but the very next moment Inga van Bronk and Peter Pilgrim come in. She's called him because she's been getting bad vibes all night; they met at Doris's funeral. Willard lives just long enough to tell the truth about himself and Julian and about Doris's murder, and Julian shoots himself. Curtain.

SIDNEY   No Scene Three?

CLIFFORD   About what? They're both dead. The play is over.

SIDNEY   Sounds a little unsatisfying. I'll be glad to think some more.

CLIFFORD *(Coming closer to* SIDNEY, *gun aimed)* No, thanks. I'll manage to fill in the holes. *(Tucks the gun in his belt and reaches into* SIDNEY*'s jacket on the desk-chair back)* And now I'm going to pack and call a taxi. *(Taking bills from* SIDNEY*'s wallet)* I'm taking whatever money I can find. *(Pockets the bills, puts the wallet on the desk, takes the handcuff key from its place on the wall and pockets it)* Before I leave, when the cab is at the door, I'll give you the key. You'll tell people that you gave me my notice and I accepted it with grace and charm. If you say I stole anything, or hassle me in any way, you'll be opening up a very messy can of peas. *(Vivid lightning, loud thunder. The lights flicker, dim, and come up again)* How about that? You've got a bit of *Angel Street* to keep you company. Maybe I'll find some rubies upstairs. See you anon.
  (He heads for the foyer, enters it, and starts up the stairs. The instant he's out of sight, SIDNEY *shucks off the cuffs, rises, takes a small armed crossbow from over the mantel, and ratcheting it, hurries to the foyer. He aims the bow up the stairs)*

SIDNEY Cliff? . . . Those *were* Houdini's. *(He fires the bow. A gunshot sounds, and then the gun is heard falling on the stairs. And then* CLIFFORD *falls, part of him coming into view.* SIDNEY, *who has retreated from the gunshot, returns and stands looking down at* CLIFFORD, *then reaches past him to pick something up. Coming back into the study, he puts the gun* CLIFFORD *used in its place. The lights dim and come up, but not quite to full.* SIDNEY *puts the cross-bow where he sat, picks up the handcuffs and puts them where they belong, picks up the gun he himself used and puts it in its place on the wall, his hand shaking. Wiping his brow, he thinks for a harried moment, then goes back to* CLIFFORD, *takes hold of him, and drags him down off the stairs and into the study, to where the ax lies. The crossbow bolt protrudes from* CLIFFORD's *chest, off-center. The lights dim further as* SIDNEY *moves* CLIFFORD *into the right position;* SIDNEY *glances anxiously at the nearest lamp)* Hang in there, Connecticut Light and Power . . . *(The lights come up a bit)* Attagirl. *(Leaving* CLIFFORD, SIDNEY *goes to the desk, takes the stack of paper, and heads for the fireplace. The lights dim further as* SIDNEY *dumps the papers into the fireplace. He crouches, takes a match, strikes it; as he lights the papers, the lights go out)* Damn. *(Now there's only the firelight as* SIDNEY *stands straight and looks around. Lightning flashes, thunder rolls.* SIDNEY *goes to* CLIFFORD, *crouches by him. The firelight grows stronger as* SIDNEY *returns to the desk and stuffs bills into his wallet and puts the wallet into his jacket. He holds the key to the handcuffs for a moment, and throws it in their general direction. Another look around, and he picks up the phone and dials Operator. He waits in the growing firelight)* Come on, come on . . . Jesus . . . Police Department. *(He waits again, silently; tears his shirt a bit more; waits, waits; then)* My name is Bruhl. I live out on Rabbit Hill Road. I just killed my secretary. He was coming at me with an ax . . . That's right. And wait till you hear this part. You're going to think I'm drunk but I'm stone-cold sober. I shot him with a medieval crossbow. It was the only thing I could get my hands on . . . *(Sits in his desk chair)* I assure you it isn't. Come on out and see. But you'd better bring some flashlights . . . B-r-u-h-l, Sidney . . . *(Smiles)* How nice of you to know. *His* name was Cli—

> *(The hand clutching his throat stops him; it pulls him backward as* CLIFFORD *comes up from behind the chair, stabbing again and again into* SIDNEY's *chest with the crossbow bolt.* CLIFFORD *stops stabbing and hauls himself erect, glassy-eyed, the bolt in his hand, his chest bloody. He crumples to the floor.* SIDNEY, *his hands to his own bloody chest, gasps and twitches and dies. Thunder, and blackout)*

The lights come up. The draperies are open; it's an overcast afternoon. The ax, the crossbow, and SIDNEY'*s jacket are gone, as well as the two bodies. The fireplace is empty. Otherwise everything is as it was.*

HELGA, *in mid-trance, stands by the chair where* MYRA *died.* PORTER *stands nearby, watching* HELGA *intently.*

HELGA They kill Mrs. Bruhl.

PORTER What? She died of a heart attack!

HELGA They . . . make it to happen. *(Holding the chair with both hands, eyes closed)* Pain she feels—is that she sees Bruhl *kill* boy.

PORTER Now, hold on a minute; the boy didn't—

HELGA *(Interrupting him)* Quiet! *(Stays in her trance)* Bruhl shows her play from boy, good play. Boy comes, Bruhl kills—around neck, tight—to take play. She helps him carry boy out. Pain brings *me*, but now I am gone—and boy is from grave! Comes with log! No! No! Please! I tried to stop—*Eiiii!* *(Winces, and lets out breath)* She dies.
(Comes out of the trance, blinks)

PORTER My God! A fake murder to bring about a real one! Are you sure that's what happened? *(*HELGA *nods, leaves the chair, is drawn to the desk)* I thought it was strange, the boy stepping in on such short notice . . .

HELGA *(At* CLIFFORD's *side of the desk)* Was *no* play.

PORTER There wasn't?

HELGA But now boy writes it . . . All they have done . . . *(Moving to* SIDNEY's *side)* Bruhl discovers . . .

PORTER I saw the boy locking his drawer!

HELGA Is afraid, Bruhl. Play will bring shame.

PORTER A play about *them?* Killing Myra?*(*HELGA *nods)* I'll *bet* he was afraid!

HELGA Pretends to help, but . . . *tricks boy to take ax* . . . *for play* . . . *and*—shoots with gun? *Ja,* but is no bullet! Boy has tricked *him,* to use to make more of play! Chains him, will go! But chains come apart!

PORTER The Houdini set!

HELGA Shoots boy with arrow! On stairs!

PORTER And drags him in and puts him by the ax!

HELGA Burns play . . .

PORTER The ashes in the fireplace!

HELGA *(Her hand on* SIDNEY's *chair)* Calls police.

PORTER And while he was speaking—

HELGA Boy pulls arrow from chest and—*(A stabbing gesture)*—attacks. Just as I saw four weeks ago . . . *(She draws a deep, spent breath)*

PORTER My *God*, what a story! It's—it's better than *The Murder Game!*

(*A thought strikes him; he ponders it, moving near* CLIFFORD'*s chair.* HELGA *looks across the desk at him*)

HELGA You are thinking—it could be play?

PORTER It has the *feel* of one, doesn't it? (*Looks around*) Everything happening in the one room . . . (*Thinks, finger-counts*) Five characters . . .

HELGA (*Looks into the distance*) *Deathtrap* . . .

PORTER Say, *that's* a catchy title. (*Thinks, wonders*) I couldn't write *Frankfurter*—but maybe I could write *Deathtrap.*

HELGA *Ja, ja,* I see theater! Inside, much applause! Outside, long line of ticket-buyers, shivering in cold!

PORTER My goodness, that's encouraging!

HELGA (*Turns to him*) But—(*Taps her chest*)—is my idea.

PORTER *Your* idea? How can you say that? It's—it was *Sidney's* idea, and the boy's! They lived it!

HELGA But if I not tell, you not know.

PORTER (*Considers the point*) That's true; I can't deny that. And you've supplied me with a title—which I may or may not use . . .

HELGA We share money half and half.

PORTER   Are you serious? I'm going to go home and work nights and weekends, for months, maybe even give up my vacation. All *you've* done is come in here and touch the furniture for two minutes. *If* I do in fact—

HELGA *(Interrupting him)*   If you not share money—I tell about telephone.

PORTER   Telephone?

HELGA *(Looking into the distance again)*   You speak through handkerchief, in high voice. Say dirty words to all your friends. *(*PORTER *blanches.* HELGA *turns to him)* For shame, a man like you, important lawyer with wife and two daughters—no, three daughters—to make such telephonings! Tsk, tsk, tsk, tsk, tsk!

PORTER *(Starts menacingly toward her)*   You interfering busybody . . .

> *(*HELGA *runs to the wall; grabs up and brandishes the dagger)*

HELGA   Be careful, knife is sharp. Amsterdam police have taught me self-defense. I warn you, I am strong and unafraid!

PORTER   Bitch! Whore! Foreign slut. Dutch pervert!

> *(The curtain falls as they circle the desk)*

About the Author

IRA LEVIN was twenty-two when he wrote his first novel, the award-winning thriller *A Kiss Before Dying,* and twenty-five when, fresh from military service, he wrote his first play, the smash-hit adaptation of Mac Hyman's *No Time for Sergeants.* In the years since, he has continued to work both sides of the literary street. His plays include the comedy hit *Critic's Choice,* the musical *Drat! The Cat!* and the thriller *Veronica's Room.* Among his novels are *Rosemary's Baby,* generally credited or blamed for having sparked the current revival of occultism; *The Stepford Wives;* and the international best seller *The Boys from Brazil.*

A native-born New Yorker, Mr. Levin is an alumnus of New York University and has three sons.